I0818982

BY EMMA COPLEY EISENBERG

The Third Rainbow Girl

Housemates

Fat Swim

FAT SWIM

FAT SWIM

FICTION

EMMA COPLEY EISENBERG

HOGARTH | NEW YORK

Hogarth
An imprint of Random House
A division of Penguin Random House LLC
1745 Broadway, New York, NY 10019
randomhousebooks.com
penguinrandomhouse.com

Grateful acknowledgment is made to Farrar, Straus and Giroux and Union Literary on behalf of the Estate of Grace Paley for permission to reprint an excerpt from "Therefore" from *Begin Again: Collected Poems* by Grace Paley, copyright © 2000 by Grace Paley. Reprinted by permission of Farrar, Straus and Giroux and Union Literary on behalf of the Estate of Grace Paley. All rights reserved.

Earlier versions of the following stories originally appeared in the following publications: "Fat Swim," *Virginia Quarterly Review* (2018); "Sundays," *Electric Literature* (2017); "Ray's Happy Birthday Bar" (originally titled "Ray's Birthday Bar"), *American Short Fiction* (2020); "The Dan Graves Situation," *Los Angeles Review of Books* (2017); "Mama," *ZYZZYVA* (2018); "I Want a Friend," *McSweeney's* (2019); "Swiffer Girl," *McSweeney's* (2020).

LIBRARY OF CONGRESS CATALOGING-IN-PUBLICATION DATA
Names: Eisenberg, Emma Copley author
Title: Fat swim / Emma Copley Eisenberg.
Description: First edition. | London; New York, NY: Hogarth, 2026.
Identifiers: LCCN 2025037763 (print) | LCCN 2025037764 (ebook) |
ISBN 9780593242261 hardcover | ISBN 9780593242278 ebook
Subjects: LCGFT: Short stories
Classification: LCC PS3605.I8278 F38 2026 (print) | LCC PS3605.I8278 (ebook) |
DDC 813/.6—dc23/eng/20250910
LC record available at https://lccn.loc.gov/2025037763
LC ebook record available at https://lccn.loc.gov/2025037764

Printed in the United States of America

1st Printing

FIRST EDITION

BOOK TEAM: Production editor: Cara DuBois • Managing editor: Rebecca Berlant • Production manager: Sandra Sjursen • Proofreaders: Julie Ehlers, Alissa Fitzgerald, Anya Getschel, Megha Jain, Tricia Wygal

Book design by Kevin Quach

The authorized representative in the EU for product safety and compliance is Penguin Random House Ireland, Morrison Chambers, 32 Nassau Street, Dublin D02 YH68, Ireland. https://eu-contact.penguin.ie

For Mollie

At that time
I had a pocketful
of excellent stones
but I was not
without sin   what
could I do but
walk heavily   heavily

—**GRACE PALEY**

CONTENTS

FAT
SWIM

FAT SWIM

Alice spots the fat women through the second-story kitchen window. It's the colors that catch her eye, the parade of bright bodies turning the corner of Forty-Ninth Street onto the avenue, then veering into the rec area that holds the pool.

It's Wednesday, early evening, so Dad is out at his feelings meeting. Alice has just turned eight and has been dragging her drumsticks over different household surfaces to see what sounds they make. The sink has been working well—a satisfying *ting, ting, ting.* Also the panes of window glass—higher, more muffled. The kitten meows on the ledge. Shush, Alice tells him, then bops him lightly on the head with a stick.

Back soon, back soon, back soon, Alice tells the kitten. The drumsticks roll off the counter and hit the parquet floor.

The public pool is on Alice's avenue in West Philadelphia, which has many trees and a lot of garbage. The sidewalks are cracked but the parking is permit-only—the old woman who lives in the purple house is the captain and she is efficient.

From the top of Alice's stoop she can clearly see the women

across the street and through the chain-link fence. The women are fat and they are swimming. Well, they are about to swim. They are taking off their jean shorts and belly shirts and fringe vests and heart-shaped sunglasses and putting their hair up into ponytails or, if they have short hair, pressing both of their hands onto their heads like a hat—a dance move. A song is playing from a radio that is attached to the motorbike of the boy who lives in the purple house. The song is a hip-hop song that has been playing all summer and even before that, in the weeks when the kids at school believed it should have been summer vacation but it was not, and the air conditioners were working at home but not at school. The fat women are Black and they are white, a thing that almost never happens in this neighborhood. They snap their fingers. They lean forward and stick out their butts, then lean back and lift their breasts to the sun, their bellies hanging over their bikini bottoms.

This is interesting to Alice because they are fat like her. As they move to the song, sometimes a swath of fat goes one way while the woman goes another. These are moves Alice, too, has sometimes done, but only alone and only in front of the mirror. Slight rolls of flesh puff out just below the elastic of their bras and gather on their backs like wings. Alice would like to run a finger through the creases this flesh makes. This is what she thinks about later, at night, in her bed with the lights out. With both hands, she holds the flap of fat where the low part of her stomach touches her thighs. She jiggles it in both hands—first together, then each hand separately—then lets it go. She pats the skin above her vagina, the part that her mother calls her FUPA, with her whole hand—once, twice. The thing that most people do not know about fat is that it is stronger than you think. It is not all softness. It bounces. It bounces back.

The following Wednesday, Alice is ready for the women. She sits a little closer, on the bottom step of her stoop, waiting for them. In addition to sexy touching, she has also been dreaming of the fat women in their bathing suits, which is how she knows the feeling she has for them is romantic. She has imagined a birthday party. It is her birthday, a pool party, and the women are her guests. There is cake and ice cream. Everyone eats as much as they want and no one asks if Alice is sure she really wants to eat that second piece. They eat the ice cream from pint cartons because it is assumed that everyone will finish their own pint. No one has to share, no one has to put the ice cream back with one bite left to avoid their mother noticing the carton is missing. Then there is dancing. The fat women compliment Alice on her moves. They say they have never seen moves like that and ask Alice to teach them. Then two women come up on either side of Alice, grab her hands, and swing her body back and forth. Then they toss her into the water and she swims and swims.

In real life, they are not dancing today. It is too hot, the women say, entirely too hot. They take their clothes off and get right in the water, either by jumping or easing themselves down the flimsy metal ladders. If they ease themselves in, their breasts are the first to float. Recently, Alice has learned that breasts are actually just sacks of fat. Her own breasts, which she has had for a year already, are also made of fat.

Strange, she thinks, the way people love breasts but hate fat. If the women jump in, they surface slowly, gasping and laughing, then move across the water slow as manatees. They circulate a beach ball, tapping it with the tips of their fingers until they get bored. It falls to the surface of the water with a light slap.

Alice sits with Dad when he gets home, munching on a crispy grilled cheese and carrots that he has grown in their garden. She knows now that carrots come from seeds and that just because the ones that come from their garden look like crooked knuckles and not like the smooth pinkie fingers from the grocery store does not mean they are bad.

How big will I get? Alice asks Dad, holding up another knobby carrot. Will I keep growing?

Dad looks up from the pile of stapled papers he is writing on. Whenever he is writing to his students, he uses the cheapest possible pen, Alice has noticed, usually the free ones from the bank near their house where the trolley stops. Dad is fat, too, but Alice's mom, Tara, who used to be Dad's wife, is not. Alice has noticed that this happens often—a fat man with a thin woman. Rarely does it go the other way around.

I don't know, Dad says. You will very likely keep growing up, vertically. I don't know if you will also keep growing out, horizontally. Do you want to?

Yes, says Alice.

Okay, says Dad.

. . .

After dinner, Alice and Dad take a walk to Fred's Water Ice across from the funeral parlor. Everything at Fred's is red metal—red metal poles to hold up awnings, red metal horses that you can ride for fifty cents. Alice gets a jumbo opaque plastic cup of black cherry water ice mixed with vanilla soft serve—a gelati! She holds it in one hand and the red metal hair of the horse in the other. Next to her, on Santa's red metal sleigh, is a little girl with her hair up in two poufs secured with bright colored balls that Alice thinks are cool. She thinks the girl is five, maybe six.

How old are you? Alice asks the girl.

Eight and a half, the girl says. But inside, I'm much older.

Me too, Alice says.

Her thighs are much bigger than the girl's, white tree trunks compared to the girl's Black branches. Does this matter? Can people be the same age but different sizes? Alice squeezes her thighs together, hard, to see if she can suffocate the metal horse. But he keeps right on bucking.

You're fat, the girl says.

I know, Alice says.

Oh, the girl says. What's your name?

Alice. But sometimes people call me Alley Cat or Topsy.

Because of your hair?

Yes.

Can I touch it?

Okay, Alice says. She is used to this from school. Curly hair like hers, so curly it sticks straight out from her head in a circle like a Truffula Tree, is interesting to people, she knows. It is interesting to Black kids, who make up most of her classmates, because it is like their hair but not like it too, and it is interesting to white kids who have straight hair for the same reason. Alice leans her head down and into the space between her horse and the girl's sleigh. The girl puts her hand into Alice's hair and moves it side to side.

Cool, the girl says.

Dad has his right leg up on the sitting part of the red metal picnic table and is leaning over it, stretching. His jumbo cup of mango water ice is empty, and the smallest bit of orange liquid puddles at the bottom. His feet are exposed in sandals that have a toe and a back but barely any sides. Alice worries about him. At night, after she has put on her pajamas, they meet in her red chair and he does the silly voices and smooths her hair away from her ears.

The girl gets off the ride and goes to take the hand of a tall man leaning against the red metal fence—her dad. Alice sees how this dad holds himself, chest a little puffed out. He moves a toothpick around in his mouth and his boots are laced up tight and right. Dad carries a canvas tote with two straps, and usually the tops of vegetables—kale, rhubarb, collards—poke up out of the bag. Alice worries that Dad is too gentle for this world. That he will not last. That one day she will wake up and wait for Dad to pour her cereal with blueberries and he will not be there.

Dad likes to say that he is a survivor, that he has survived many things. Alice does not know what feelings he goes to talk about on Wednesday nights, but she suspects it has something to do with this. One thing he survived is his parents. His dad, who is dead, used to put his hand on top of the television when he came home to see if Dad had been watching it. If he had been watching it, his dad would beat him, or sometimes not, but the possibility was always there. His mom lives with other old people in a facility in Florida and sometimes sends letters that arrive in manila envelopes because they are too long to be folded in three and mailed in a regular envelope. Alice has never met her.

Another thing Dad survived is Mom, who is not gone, only living in the suburbs with her new husband. Alice spends every weekend there. There is little to report because everyone is so little. Mom has shrunk even further. Mom's new husband runs marathons, leaving the house before Alice wakes up and returning halfway through the day in small shorts and shellacked with sweat. Fifteen miles! Twenty-seven miles! Mom high-fives him and then they both want to high-five Alice. Her chest starts to feel tight before dinnertime because there is usually not enough food and she usually goes to bed hungry. This tight feeling sticks around long after the meal has happened and even through the morning when she can eat again. At Mom's house, even the air feels thin.

Penny for your thoughts, Dad says, from the red table.

I'm in love, Alice says.

What news, Dad says. Who with?

I'm not sure, Alice says. I don't know their names.

You're in love with more than one person?

Yes.

Okay, Dad says. He tosses his empty cup into the red trash can. It's nice to be in love, Dad says, as they walk home. And even nicer when someone is in love with you. When your mom was in love with me, I felt good all the time. I would wake up in the morning and jump out of bed.

That night after Dad reads her the story of the princess who rescues the prince from the tower, Alice is almost asleep when she hears Dad crying on the other side of the wall. At first it is quiet, like *sniff, sniff, sniff,* but then it is louder and then very loud, as if Dad doesn't think Alice can hear him, or does not care.

On the third Wednesday, Alice starts prepping early. She digs her bathing suit out of a garbage bag that sits under many other garbage bags, from that time last summer when Dad thought they had bedbugs. Now, she is ready. She goes down the steps, looks both ways, and waits for a lowrider to pass, trundling slow. Then she crosses the street, steps up onto the sidewalk, and presses her nose through the chain-link fence.

She hears the women before she sees them. They're rounding the corner together.

And he was like—

Too hot, hot enough to roast—

What a fucking jerk—

Broke down, broke—

They carry big beach bags and walk the length of the fence, past Alice and then through the gate where a young man with a clipboard sitting on a folding chair watches them enter and nods. The pool is small, no Olympians here, but big enough to have parts of it cordoned off by plastic buoys for lap swimming. It is surrounded by ten steps of asphalt on all sides, then patchy tufts of grass. She has never come here without Dad and a sign says this is not allowed. *Child*—what a word! Though perhaps she is not supposed to notice, Alice has noticed: there is no one more unfree in this world than a child.

Alice watches, her hands holding the chain link, as the five fat women take over the corner to her left, putting their bags on the grass and spreading their towels. They take off their shirts and push them through the holes in the fence and there are those back rolls again. One of the women, Black, in a cactus-print bikini, who carries all her weight in the parts of her body covered by the bikini bottom, sees Alice looking at her and smiles, then turns when one of the other women calls her name. The other woman is white. She leans her bike up against the chain-link fence and then lifts off her loose dress to reveal a floral one-piece and thick arms. She cocks her head and winds an elastic around the bottom of her thin braid. She wants her friend to put sunscreen on her back, in the cutout below the swimsuit's top clasp but above her butt, where she can't reach. There is music from someone's phone, slow with no words, just the same beat over and over again.

The guy with the clipboard gets up to talk to a girl in a pink bikini over by the showers and this is Alice's moment; she powerwalks through the gate and over to where the fat women have put their towels. Underneath her overalls she is wearing her multicolored swimsuit. She feels the effects of the elastic fabric—how taut it is and the shimmery sensation it gives where it contacts the denim of her overalls. As she walks, she pooches out her stomach and feels its new smoothness, her rolls of fat now one continuous curve. She pats her stomach a few times. She can feel how it moves, how the impact of her hand reverberates through her flesh. She takes off her overalls and spreads them on the ground like a towel.

The sunblocked pair of women are sitting on the lip of the pool, waving their legs in the water, while the other three swim around each other. Alice walks over and stands next to the duo on the pool's edge. She feels sure they will tell her to go away but they don't. They keep on chatting, talking about a man the Black woman had been dating but was dating no longer.

He did what? honked the white woman, splashing with her feet.

The picture was right there on his phone, said the Black woman. How's that for stupid?

Alice is still standing there.

Hi, the Black one says then, shading her eyes from the sun when she looks up at Alice.

Hi, says Alice.

The two women look at each other a minute.

Want to sit with us? the Black woman says.

Alice's chest gets tight, but not like at Mom's house. More like balloon tight, tight like the head of the drums they play in music class.

Okay, Alice says.

I like your suit, the white one says, leaning forward. It's pretty.

Thanks, Alice says.

We've seen you, the Black one says. You live across the street?

That's right, Alice says. That's me.

. . .

Before long, all five of the women are in the water and it is time for Alice to get in too. She eases herself down the ladder, pushes out against the wall with her feet, and does a fast doggy paddle. She can swim only medium well. The beach ball appears and Alice has trouble hitting it with her hands while also staying afloat because she is so much shorter than the women.

Oh, oh, one of them says, noticing, so they move their game into the shallower end. Now Alice is having fun. She dives for the ball and hits it just before it smacks the surface of the water. The women laugh and clap. They take a page from her book and are soon diving for the ball too. Alice bounces up and down on the balls of her feet, ready to jump at any moment.

After a while, the women get out of the pool and go lie on their towels. Alice lies on her overalls.

The women are talking about leg hair and armpit hair and the individual decisions they make about it.

One woman, a white woman with a shaved head, says that a long time ago she decided she no longer cared what the world thought. Fuck it, she says. Her leg hair is very long and Alice can see individual hairs beginning to come unstuck from her wet skin as the sun dries her body.

Want to touch it? the woman says to the group, and they all do. Want to touch it? she says to Alice. Alice does. It feels soft like the caterpillars that Alice sometimes finds growing on Dad's carrots in the garden. But more importantly, though the woman's calf is fat like Alice's, it does not feel the same. Where

Alice's calves are mushy, this woman's leg is firm, with the mark of a round muscle, large as a grapefruit, beneath the skin.

The Black woman in the cactus bikini—Bree, someone calls her—starts reading palms.

Want me to do yours? she asks Alice. She takes Alice's hand. Hmm, she says.

Alice feels each of Bree's individual fingers, which are pretty and manicured with thick yellow nail polish, move over the skin of her hand. Later, when Alice wants to feel the good sexy feelings, she will think of Bree.

You're going to live a long time, Bree says. See this line? She traces the line that goes from the bottom of Alice's index finger diagonally down to where it meets her wrist. But, Bree says, you will suffer.

Suffer? Alice asks. She has heard the word—once, a few times.

It means, says Bree, that life will not be easy for you. There will be—how can I say it? Challenges.

Don't tell her that, says the white woman with the back cutout. She's only a child.

Why not? Bree says. She needs to know.

The women lie down on their backs and get very quiet. The sun is very hot. Alice stays sitting up a minute to survey the bodies around her. Their breasts look very nice, snuggled up inside the cups of their bright bathing suits. Alice feels strong, up for any challenge. She shimmies her shoulders a little and wiggles her toes. She lies down on her back too. The air moves fast across her wet arms. The clouds move fast across the sky.

. . .

Back at home, after they've all parted ways and promised to see each other next Wednesday, Alice lets the kitten walk all over her chest, lets it knead her flesh with its paws because it thinks she is its mother. *Meow, meow,* it says. It leaves little red claw marks on her breasts. It jumps onto a shelf and begins to play with the glass jar of rocks that Alice and Dad carried for miles along the shore of Martha's Vineyard.

The kitten pushes the jar of rocks with its paw just as Alice hears Dad's footsteps on the landing. The jar hits the floor with a loud bang, but the glass is thick and it only rolls across the hardwood without breaking.

Jesus, Dad says when he is standing in the doorway, Jesus Christ. His face looks red and smushed, less defined than usual. He shrugs off his tote bag onto a kitchen chair.

He bends down and picks up the jar very slowly, as if it takes all of his energy.

Why are you wet? Dad asks Alice. There are little puddles on the floor under her feet and her butt is leaving a dark spot on the patterned sheet that covers the couch.

Where do you go on Wednesday nights? Alice asks back.

Dad stands for a moment, moves a hand to his hip, then drops the hand.

Alice, Dad says. Answer me. Why are you wet?

I went to the pool.

Alone? That was dangerous, Alice. I'm disappointed in you.

Maybe, Alice says slowly, I am disappointed in *you*. Why do you cry at night? Is it because you suffer?

With his whole palm, Dad runs a hand down his face, wiping it of expression. He takes off his sandals and for once just throws them by the door instead of placing them neatly in the shoe rack as he is always reminding Alice to do.

There are things in this world that are too cruel to tell a child, he says. Even a great one like you.

What things? Alice says.

I'm going to take a shower, Dad says.

They have dinner and it is fine. Everything is fine. Dad is his usual self again, smiling and counting his peas into groups of five so they can practice multiplication tables. In the red chair, he does the silly voices. He says nothing more about the pool, neither forgiving Alice nor forbidding her from returning.

Good night, good night, Dad says, and flicks off the unicorn lamp. The hall light is still on, and Alice can hear Dad moving around the apartment.

Alice's vagina hurts, in that dull achy good kind of way. She thinks about Bree in the cactus bikini, but does not touch.

Outside the window that holds her air-conditioning unit, the summer wind blows. Alice feels very awake, her eyes cutting the dark. She can see the outline of every object in her room—the poster of Emma Goldman with her little glasses and the book about the wild horse who lives on an island called Chincoteague and the jar of rocks that Dad must have brought into her bedroom by mistake.

That day in Martha's Vineyard, they walked a long time collecting rocks before the thunder came. They had to do the whole walk in reverse in the rain but eventually made it back to the car and Dad gave her his big orange sweatshirt with the oversized hood.

I love you, Dad said.

I know, Alice said. But you don't love you.

I know, Dad said. His hands were on the wheel but the car was off. It was raining louder than it had ever rained. I'm working on it, Dad said. I'm going as fast as I can.

Go faster, Alice said.

Alice has a feeling then, lying in the dark in her bed, and the feeling is like a presence, or a spirit, like how people describe their spirits leaving their body when they are dying. But the spirit seems to be coming from the outside, from the night, from the street that lies between her and the pool, and it seems to want to tell her something of the future, to make her know that though she is good now, and though she has already done better than her parents, the world is still waiting to tell her who she is and what her body means.

She still has the rest of the summer, three months of Wednesdays. The women are there every week, without fail. They buy her ice cream and teach her how to whip it and how to lean back, how to crack her back and how to crack her knuckles, how to whistle and how to snap, how to spit and how to make a man who calls out to her on the street wish he had never been born.

The spirit knocks at the windowpane—once, twice, three times. Alice is gripped then, suddenly afraid.

Go away, go away, go away, she says to the spirit. And for now, it does.

SUNDAYS

You want to know what I think about knuckle tattoos, about getting the words BOTH WAYS inked across your fingers, oriented so you can read it instead of the world. There is a man I know who can do it, though he says it will not be easy. There will be plastic gloves involved; you will have to be so gentle with your hands for such a long time.

I understand what you are getting at. When I was a child, my parents would pause me on the corner of Fifth Avenue, metal bubby cart full of greens. Do you want to go to the bakery with Dad or back to the apartment with Mom? Sometimes we dawdled there thirty or forty minutes while I looked between their faces, the cabs rushing south.

I want both cake and pie, to live by the ocean and in an ocean of strangers. One day I stick a jumbo yellow barrette in my hair, pair it with a white cotton sundress; the next I'll pull on Carhartt work pants and a sleeveless muscle tee. I do not mix and match, I do not mash up. I separate, alternate, switch, repeat.

Is this too much chaos? The world says yes, but I say no. There is something delicious in putting two things that should be kept apart right up next to each other. For example, in the late afternoon, putting your hand inside a girl who is saying *Oh shit* into your neck, and then, at dusk, putting your face into the crevasse made by two pillows as a man pushes into you, saying these same words again and again. During the subway ride between them, you repeat in your mind the word *untenable.* In Philadelphia, the El train hurtles aboveground, past American flags painted on carpet factories and the four-lane Interstate 95, which you have traveled in every season and in every kind of weather. I like that word—*untenable.* It means impossible to hold on to with your hands. It doesn't mean impossible.

I don't know if this is a story because what has happened so far may not be connected to what is coming. For a long time I lost the word *story,* and am only now getting it back. I have discovered there are reasons why the world does not make bothness easy, why we are told, *You can't have your cake and eat it too.* This way of living is not for the faint of heart. It's vain and detail-oriented work. A lot of looking in the mirror. A lot of hedging your bets—you can cut your hair short, but if you do, be prepared to wear dangly earrings. It requires carrying with you only what can fit in a backpack, and a great deal of advance planning.

Let's start at the beginning of the week, with Jeffrey, a grad student at the City University who I see on Mondays and Thursdays in my neighborhood—West Philly. I have never seen the inside of his apartment though I know which window it is and walk by it often on my way to get beer. He appears at my door in old white sneakers and later, after he leaves, will jog eight miles in the dark. At first this disappointed me for I thought he would be a man good for quiet trouble, down to drink many beers on many porches and roam these cracked streets for hours in summer while we talked about music and movies and God and made out on a basketball court. He had gone to Oberlin after all. He says the jogging is his Asian side, and the studying philosophy and making no money is the white one.

I cook him pasta, pork chops, black rice. This is good, Jeffrey says, using his bony index finger to wipe the plate clean. He does the dishes, then runs his hands through his hair, which sticks up like a cartoon of a hedgehog, a cartoon of a boy. I've patched the elbows on two of his button-ups. There's nothing to be done about the threadbare T-shirts but throw them away. After dinner, we sit on my porch steps so he can smoke and I can watch the boys bouncing basketballs. His big knees rise nearly to his chest. We talk to my neighbor who works as an orderly at the hospital down the block. We talk about the little girl who died at the school nearby because there was no school nurse that day and about how there is still no school nurse there. I take some pleasure in how my neighbor sees us—two kids sitting close together on a stoop.

Fatima is Tuesday and Wednesday nights, half an hour east by train. She lives in a group house of queer Muslims close to the Fishtown gym where I box, which is how we met. We were assigned to hold the bag for each other at my first class. I fretted about kicking her in the face; she didn't. As she jabbed and cross-kicked, I absorbed the bag absorbing her. She wore a hijab and athletic shorts—crimson mesh with white piping, the colors of an elite education.

So, I said, over whiskeys at one of the brew pubs in her neighborhood, how is it that you worship Allah and also fuck women?

I think she got up right then.

Sorry, I said. My obsession with seemingly contradictory things can make me rude.

She sat down. And racist, she said. Don't ever make me explain myself to you again.

For the rest of the date, we talked about a famous female Black musician and a famous Black actress and whether or not they were dating. She said they were, and I said they weren't. She was right. It took us months to kiss more than a peck.

Are you attracted to me? I asked finally.

Yes, Fatima said. Oh yes.

Now she gets excited just touching the edge of my skirt in a movie theater or the strap of my purple backpack at a lecture. Underneath her hijab, her hair is short and unbrushed. I feel ashamed to know this, as if underneath is not what I should be cherishing.

Fatima and her housemates sit on aluminum barstools around a large kitchen island and eat bowls of expensive blueberry ice cream. I try to remember what I learned in tenth-grade social studies when we did religions of the world, the Five Pillars of Islam. Only one comes back to me—*There is no god but you God.*

The conclusion her housemates reach: Islam and fucking women are contradictory, but so what?

Fatima's friend, also a scientist, kills the end of the pint.

Has anyone ever died from living in a contradiction? this friend asks.

Definitely, Fatima says.

Memory: My father getting ready for court. He calls my name and I come to where he is seated at my mother's dressing table. He is color-blind and needs help. Does this go? he asks, holding up a red tie to a white shirt. Sure, I say. No, he says. It either does or it doesn't. He is defending a man who killed his wife then put her body in the furnace of their apartment building. But he loved his dog, my father tells me as he is leaving, showing me a picture of his client standing next to a German shepherd with extremely large paws.

I slip down into Fatima's white cotton comforter, into sleep, underneath the memory, underneath my mother's dressing table. In the dark green carpet are seashells that rattle when I pick them up. I keep rattling one and waiting for the thing that is doing the rattling to emerge from the shell, but nothing emerges. I wake to Fatima praying on the floor facing the bay windows to the east; see the exposed soles of her feet. She chants words that I have learned mean *peace* and *blessings upon you,* that mean *mercy.* She touches her forehead to the carpet.

Beth is how I began loving this way—simultaneously. My Fridays and Saturdays, she calls herself a mama's boy. In her rambling stone house in Mount Airy where she lives with her forever partner who looks just like her but taller, she has a wall of snapback hats. She doesn't believe in microwaves but believes very much in gyms, and in suffering for results. She still has a flip phone. As I drive the switchbacks into the Pocono Mountains, she yells at inept residents, discussing medical conditions with intimidating acronyms. She is a pulmonologist who also makes art pieces out of wooden boxes filled with tiny objects—metal soldiers, trilobites, miniature Slinkies. If you met her, you would want her. Most people do.

We have picked blueberries in the woods on the highest peak in West Virginia, we have lain with our spines against wood planks on the deck of a stilted house in coastal Mississippi while mosquitoes sucked on our toes and ears. Beth says, Relationship structure. She says, Just tell me what you need. There came a certain point, she says, where I realized I could not just sit back and say, My girlfriend is killing me. She holds my hand and rubs my palm as if she is about to read it. In bed, she scoots her face an inch from mine and keeps it that way all night. I breathe slowly and lie awake. In pictures of her from childhood, Beth is thin in a striped bikini, squinting hard at the camera in an expression that might be crank or might be rage—as if the camera clicked just before she could scream.

Sunday mornings arrive bright and groggy with too much coffee and not enough dreaming. I drive I-95 up or down the

East Coast from wherever I have been with Beth. I listen to the radio, to audiobooks, and talk to my friends from college on the phone. They live in Portland, San Francisco, Austin; they work, they marry. Why Philadelphia? they say. I just like it here, I say. I like its attitude, I say, and its spirit. But I'm tired, I say. Too much traveling, they say. Stay home. They talk to me about the briefs they are filing, the emails they are answering, the art they are making—huge canvases full of nothing but red, nothing but blue, real gold leaf on top of faux gold leaf. One sweet friend, a nurse, keeps me from falling asleep by describing the latest videos I've missed—the president unable to say the letter *H,* a man who built a palace for his cat entirely from cardboard boxes.

I believe there are a few places you can go where contradiction doesn't matter, where logic isn't anything, where the sum is always more than zero, but I have never found them. Finding them is a useless line of thinking—that much I can report back. You miss a lot in the searching. It takes time to be in transit; I am often already gone, but not yet arrived. It's possible that when you build your body for too many people at once, no one comes to see it.

At least I can say I tried. At least I can say I've found a way to live free one day a week. On Sundays, I park my little pickup truck on the street where my neighbor's son has opened the fire hydrant. I fling open the door to my house and let the mail that has accumulated fall to the tiled vestibule floor. I sit down on a chair and, because there is nothing to do, I do nothing. Don't think, don't remember, don't dream.

And then it's dawn; not quite Monday. Beth has texted:

good night with a GIF of a person sleeping in old-fashioned pajamas. Fatima is on her knees, facing the light. Jeffrey is smoking a cigarette and drinking coffee. Soon he will go to work in his one tie, and then he'll be at my door again.

I wonder if BOTH WAYS are really the words you want. I wonder if what you want is words.

The skin of my left hand can't take tattoos. The flesh there, particularly along the knuckles, got puffed and scarred from the tailpipe of a Cameroonian motorbike the summer I turned twenty-one. The motorcycle was borrowed, but driven by a man I was sleeping with who had grown up thirty minutes inland but never left his hometown. That day, we rode to the shore, and he nudged the bike down into the sand. I watched him see the ocean for the first time, watched him wade in very slowly to his ankles and then turn back to me. I thought he would be happy, but he wasn't—he was afraid. My mistake was reaching down toward the motorcycle's saddlebag for the camera, thinking then he would have to smile.

My hand! I cried out, it's ruined now.

My friend laughed. That will hurt like a mother, he said. And it will last forever.

RAY'S HAPPY BIRTHDAY BAR

At Ray's Happy Birthday Bar, we specialize in birthdays. A free shot for you if you can show me a driver's license that proves it's your birthday, two free ones if the address on said license is South Philadelphia, and if you're a lifer with ten years or more of loyal patronage, the number's three and Ray will turn on the disco ball. I read somewhere that you have to get twenty-three people in the same room before there is a fifty percent chance that two of them will have the same birthday. Here the odds are much better.

It's Sunday, early, and no one is at the bar for Gin's party yet except me and a lifer named Wade and Ray's boxer terrier, who sleeps on the one city-mandated air vent.

There was my fortieth when it hailed, Wade says. He owns the hardware store across the street and never charges me to cut a key when I lose mine.

I remember, I say. Ray bought pizza.

That was my favorite birthday, Wade says. He wipes a hand across his new neck tattoo of bleeding thorns, and a little real blood comes away on his palm.

A birthday boy with a ponytail comes in and sits at the

disco-ball end of the bar. His Texas driver's license has him with a crew cut and the name John.

What'll it be, John? I say.

It's Tex, he corrects. Take one for yourself, he says, and slides a fiver across the bar.

I do like the man says, and it makes Gin's party ride a little lighter knowing I have a date if I want one.

However, says Wade, another contender was the birthday my cat killed a crow in the street and all the kids from St. Mary's came over to see. Thirty-four, I think, because I still had that Ford Ranger and the PPA towed it. Gin went and got it back from the yard as a gift.

Gin's good like that, I say.

Tex's shirt has pearl buttons and I imagine the appealing sound they would make when unsnapped.

My roommate, Gin, I tell him. It's her thirtieth we're celebrating tonight. Though her birthday's not technically till tomorrow.

Thirty, Tex says, and whistles unsuccessfully.

Hence Gin quitting smoking, Wade says. And the new girlfriend.

Not necessarily, I say. Remember the kale soup diet? And the book-a-week plan?

Gin is prone to these bettering binges, so when she woke me up on a Monday a month ago to ask my opinion on her answers for the dating app, I didn't think anything of it. Mondays are our day, the only day off we share.

Wade was in my bed, gauged earlobes swinging.

You like that? Wade wanted to know, cock in hand. I was

medium horny so I said, Sure, and he put my head in the sour part of his inner thigh where it said DONNA in thick cursive ink. Then Gin started pounding on my door.

Go away! I called. I'm sleeping!

Tracy, Gin said. I could feel her leaning her forehead against her side of the door.

I need your help, she said.

Gin was in pajama pants and a tank that showed off her arms, her hair up in oily cowlicks. I sent Wade out to ShopRite for cut-and-bake cinnamon rolls, and Gin lay down on my bed with her feet hanging off and talked to me while I straightened my hair. She was talking about quitting her job as the manager of a bougie Rittenhouse seafood restaurant. She was talking about joining the Peace Corps.

I do love to travel, she said. Also, look who I found online!

Her high school girlfriend from Ohio.

I said, Jesus, Gin, she's married now. She's got a kid.

I know, Gin said. But. I want someone, she said. I'm tired of bar whores.

You wanna go to Passion Palace? I have a date with that drummer tonight and could use your opinion. To garter belt or not to garter belt?

I want a girl, Gin said. A nice girl.

What makes you think a nice girl would want you? I said. OK, I said.

They were in here the other night, Wade says. Very lovey.

Rachel, I say. Her name is Rachel.

I get the plastic bag of limes from the backup fridge and start cutting and stacking the wedges in a Tupperware.

She's a lawyer, Wade says, to my tits, which are shaking slightly from the lime cutting.

She's a vegan, I say. And basically Thumbelina.

Rachel is actually miniature. I was the only witness to Gin and Rachel's first date, just two days after Gin made her dating app debut.

Rachel's legs did not touch the ground nor the stool's footrest when she sat at the bar.

Justice, Rachel said. Philadelphia Cyclist Bill of Rights, she said, sipping a craft beer I had to go to the basement to dig up. She kept wiping her eyes.

It's a little smoky in here, she said.

I could see Gin's fingers tapping against the pack in her front pocket where a corner had worn through the denim, but she didn't light up. Rachel used her hands a lot when she talked, and asked a lot of questions.

I am, Gin said. I do. I remember when. I don't know. Maybe someday.

Gin made a big show of buying Rachel's one beer and holding the door open for her on the way out, and when Gin waved goodbye to me it was clear where their night was headed. But when I got back to our rowhome around three, there were none of the telltale signs that Gin was entertaining a lady guest—no crusty pans from late-night fried-egg sandwiches in the sink or trampy heels upside down on the living room carpet or music blasting from upstairs. The house was quiet, just the cars honking outside. A pair of brown leather sandals sat neatly lined up on the landing outside Gin's door when I went past it on the way up to my room.

Rachel's sandals were there again the next week when I came back from Tantrum with the drummer. In the club he'd been hot, insinuating his leg between mine on the dance floor, but when we paused on the landing outside Gin's room, he got tentative as a teenager.

Jesus, I said. I peeled my shirt off and threw it over the banister. I thought I heard little feet behind Gin's door, but it stayed closed.

In the morning, I woke up too early to the sound of Gin laughing.

That's not what that word means! That tickles!

Gin laughing and laughing.

Later, smoking out my window, I saw Rachel put on her slick silver helmet and climb aboard her yellow bike, which she'd locked up on our gate next to the plastic Virgin Mary statues left over from the grandmother who rented this place before us. Rachel plopped herself over the curb and into our narrow street, cutting off a pickup truck mid-acceleration. The pickup honked and slammed on its brakes, but Rachel didn't even look. The truck crawled along behind her, pushing up against her back wheel, then the driver stuck out his head.

Come on, he said. Bitch, he said.

Rachel's wheels tick-ticked evenly toward the intersection of our street with Washington Avenue, her feet slowing down into the yellow light. But then, just as the light turned red, she stood up on her pedals and raced through it.

. . .

Ray comes through the silver tinsel curtain so suddenly that I drop the frozen dinner I was about to nuke. He holds a rack of pint glasses tight against his red Phillies T-shirt.

Whadja bring me today? Ray wants to know.

He puts the aluminum pan of brownies on the bar in front of Wade and they go at it with butter knives.

My favorite birthday is not my own, Ray says. Ten years ago today. This girl.

He puts his arm low around my waist where my jeans begin and smacks his Marlboro Menthol Light lips on the side of my face.

What what? Tex wants to know.

He unsnaps two pearl buttons and rolls up his sleeves to the elbow. Already, he wants all our stories.

On the same day, what are the odds, that fool Gin, and Tracy here, both come into my bar, Ray says. Tracy fresh off the bus from Camden. She didn't even smoke, this one.

I did so, I say to Tex.

You did not so, Ray says.

Alright, I say, and light a cigarette as if to make up for the past. But you had that sign.

I'd been pounding pavement for three weeks after getting fired from my job sponge-bathing a girl named Serena. We'd done crossword puzzles and I'd lent her a plaid skirt so we could match as we danced, but then her brother got out of the marines and was hot, so that ended. But Serena had called me Pretty Girl, as in, *Hey hey Pretty Girl more apple juice!*, so when I saw the sign in the window of Ray's Happy Birthday Bar that said PRETTY GIRL BARTENDER WANTED, I guessed it was divine intervention.

Ray says, That's when I was married, thank Jesus no more to What's-Er-Name. That sign was her idea. But anyway. Tracy walks into the bar. She is wearing this very ugly coat, made of sheeps. But she is very beautiful. But she says she doesn't smoke, so What's-Er-Name doesn't want to hire her. After all, then, now, Ray's is a smoking bar.

Praise the lord, Wade says.

Never will I cave to the city, Ray says. Here, we sit inside like human beings. Anyway, Tracy is about to leave when the door opens and in comes this girl, definitely underage. So skinny, like a little boy.

I picture Gin as she was then: jeans hanging off her lack-of-an-ass (too much meth), her hair short as a man's on the sides but long on top. She carried a green tube-shaped rucksack swung jauntily over her shoulder like she was the first little pig off to make her fortune.

So, Ray says, Gin orders a beer. I look at her license, she does not even try to present false ID and she is only nineteen. What came over me? I do not know. I have always liked the name Virginia. I gave this Gin a shot of Jäger. Free, I said. Because it is your birthday and because I have this beautiful woman in my bar, but only because, do not be coming back in here again, I said. And then Tracy said, Is that your golden rule? Is that why you are called Ray's Happy Birthday Bar? I said, That is just the concept which every bar should have. Happy is the concept. What does birthday mean if it does not mean happy? But it occurs. I think for a second. That is not bad. One free shot. Who can have just one? So Ray's Birthday Rules are born. And I hire this Tracy on the spot even though she will not smoke and is soon pregnant as a pumpkin.

That sinks into the air for a second.

You have a kid? Wade says. There goes my fantasy.

Ray gives me the teeth grimace he makes when What's-Er-Name comes around the bar asking why she's still getting his cable bill in the mail.

Correction, I say. Had. That's what nice Catholic adoptions are for.

His name is Jake, Ray says. One time, we are driving by his house in Lansdowne.

Alright, I say.

Tex turns to me, says, But what was your favorite birthday?

The bar is filling up. I do a couple of other birthday freebies: a barrel-shaped woman with pigtails, and a men's hockey team whose birthday boy leans so far over the bar in my direction that I have to stand back by the microwave to pour his shot. Gin's employees from the seafood restaurant start to show up, and for them I do mostly Sunday night specials.

Where's Gin? Gin's gay boy assistant manager asks, washing his Jäger down with a swig of PBR.

She'll be here, I say.

Your hair's different, he says. It's purple.

Very astute, I say.

On a whim this afternoon before work, Gin and I decided to dye a streak of my hair, so out Gin went to ShopRite. I was in my bathroom putting on my face when I heard the plastic bags coming up my stairs. She mixed the bleach as I did eye shadow and lipstick. While the purple seeped in, I sat on the tile in a towel and she sat in the doorway and we watched movie trailers about the end of the world.

This is nice, Gin said. We haven't done this in forever.

You got a girlfriend, I said.

I did, she said. But before that, even then we didn't.

Summertime is hermit time, I said. My room. The only functioning AC.

I know, she began. My birthday. It brings Jake with it. You're thinking about him.

I said, So what? So I think about him.

She said, Every year on my birthday, we do the same thing. I make you breakfast and get Vince and Courteney's address out of the drawer with the menus and put it by your breakfast plate, and then I put it away after you've looked at it for a while, and then we walk down the block to get ice cream at the Custard Shack but end up drunk at Ray's.

I know, I said. I stood and unwrapped the towel so Gin could see my body. It's magical.

Gin looked for a second, then turned her head.

Then she said, What if we did something else?

I turned on the water and dragged the curtain. From the sound of her breathing, Gin was still there when the purple started running.

. . .

Ray's bell clanks when Gin comes into the bar. Gin's hair is slicked down and she is in suspenders and a checkered button-up that pulls apart to show the too-tight sports bra she uses to strap down her tits. I have often said that Gin would be the perfect guy if she were not a woman.

My my, Miss Virginia, I say.

The bell clanks again. Gin takes Rachel's tiny hand and pulls Rachel up to sit on the stool beside her. Rachel's long, curly brown hair is up in a ponytail. It's so dark it's almost black like mine but is too shiny to be dyed. She wears a purple cotton dress and no makeup.

Madam, Gin says. Two of your finest shots of alcohol.

Actually, it's three, I say. You're a lifer now. Ray, if you please.

Ray pulls the string. The disco ball is the size of an apple and it spins slowly, casting little dots on the cigarette machine near the bathroom and on Tex's face. He has a face like a friend. I put the shots in front of Gin.

You better not try to come back in and get three more tomorrow, I say. I know where you live!

Oh, get a room! Wade says, *haha*-ing.

Hey Gin, I say, for old time's sake and because Tex hasn't heard this one either. Remember that time we fucked?

Gin sits very still. Nope, she says.

Rachel takes her hair down from its ponytail, then gathers it back up again.

I don't remember, Gin says. We were so drunk.

That's putting it extremely mildly, I say.

It was Gin's twenty-sixth birthday and there was a piñata in the shape of a pair of oversized tits and a kissing competition that had Gin pressed up against Wade's whip-creamed mouth. Gin was between, and obliging girl that I am, I didn't want her to go without on her birthday. In the morning it was sunny, and Gin kissed and kissed the side of my face like a dog.

Wake up, wake up, Gin said, jumping out of bed. She lifted the black towels from my windows. Her ass was flat and white. She said, Wake up! You'll sleep your life away.

Rachel lifts a square white box out of a paper bag and sets it on the bar.

Cake! she says. From that little bakery that always has the line around the block.

I made brownies, I say.

We'll have yours first, she says, then takes her cake out of its box.

Tex keeps buying me drinks, I keep buying Gin drinks, and Gin keeps buying Rachel drinks. Rachel is slow, and Gin helps her finish. Rachel keeps taking the inside of her wrist and wiping it across her eyes.

Gin gets up to go to the cigarette machine. I say, Buy me a pack?

No, she says. I'm just peeing. I told you, I quit.

And then I know it's serious. As long as I have known her, Gin has been a world-class smoker.

I didn't see Gin for six months after that day we met and then she showed up at the bar again, a pack rolled in the sleeve of her white T-shirt, James Dean style.

Ray told you not to come back in here, I said.

I know, she said. But I just moved to Philadelphia for good and I remembered this bar. She smiled through her bangs and said, Show me around?

I told Ray I was going out for a smoke break. We crossed the triangle intersection where the vinyl sign on the chain-link fence says LOOKING FOR GOOD PEOPLE MAY HAVE BAD CREDIT, and passed the row of houses with white iron gates that all have the same blond wood front doors and the same three paces of patchy grass and porcelain Jesus and Madonna figurines in their yards. We stood in front of DeFalco & Sons funeral parlor, where a heart-shaped flower arrangement was losing its blue and white carnations into the street.

Who dies here, do you think? Gin said.

Us, probably, I said, and headed off toward the line at Pat's.

Girl can eat, Gin said, once I'd gotten my two cheesesteaks and we were sitting at one of the red metal tables on the street.

You know, I said. I'm eating for two, as they say.

Oh, Gin said. Oh wow, she said.

So there's that. But lucky for this man-child, I have selected a wholesome Catholic couple from the internet.

Gin said, Can I see?

I laughed. You want to see *Vince and Courteney, College-*

Educated, Loving Catholics, But Sorry Absolutely No Birth-Parent Contact?

Gin put down her steak and thought about it. Yes, she said.

This, I think, is the moment where Gin signed up.

OK, I said.

OK, she said.

Without Gin, Rachel takes her beer and moves off into the crowd. Gin's assistant manager climbs into the wooden booth by the window and sets up a kind of DJ station with some speakers and his phone. He puts on a song and raises his hands above his head, and soon Wade and some roller derby girls and Gin's other coworkers are dancing too.

Go on, Ray says to me, and he takes over the bar.

When Gin comes out of the bathroom, right away she wants to know where Rachel is.

Who knows, she could be anywhere, I say, and hunch down like a munchkin.

That's not funny, Gin says.

It's a little bit funny, I say. I turn back to Ray. Another shot for my tall friend, I say.

No, Gin says. I shouldn't. Rachel's leaving for a conference tomorrow and she'll be gone all week.

What is alcohol for if not for sex? I say.

Gin gives me a look then, a look like the deliveryman from Pho 75 gives me when I pay him in one-dollar bills.

I used to think that too, Gin says.

Then Gin spots Rachel and goes to her. They dance to a

slow song. It's a good song, one of the old bluesmen my aunt used to try to get her choir to sing.

Gin's hands. They are big and good and all the same thickness even through the knuckles. Gin's hands start out on the back of Rachel's neck where there are dark curly baby hairs underneath her ponytail. Then they wipe across Rachel's bare shoulders and move down along her hairy arms until they pull Rachel's wrists in to rest against the part of Gin's chest where it is flat like a man's. The two of them dance so slow, the slowest kind of dance you've ever seen.

Gin's assistant manager is jabbing his phone with the tip of his index finger, scrolling powerfully.

Hey man, I say. Can't you give us something with a beat?

He raises an eyebrow but does it, putting on something faster and newer. It's almost midnight. Ray's boxer terrier stands up from the air vent and shakes off her sleep. Rachel and Gin step back from each other, and everyone who was too embarrassed to slow dance jumps back out onto the floor.

Here we go, I say, and pull Tex up from his stool and we get wild. I stomp on the floor with the heels of my boots and Tex hooks his thumbs into my belt loops and lifts me up. But when I turn around, Gin is dancing behind me and Rachel is nowhere and Gin and I jump up and down, hitting the balloons that float near the bar's low ceiling. I lean into Gin then, only a little, so it's just the edges of our clothing touching. I light a cigarette and hand it to Gin. She looks at it in between her fingers and takes a small puff and then a long drag. I hold the cigarette above the crowd and Gin and I press our foreheads into each other as we jump, her sweat-slicked forehead to my foundation-gunked one.

When I was pushing Jake out of my vagina, the only person there in the room with me besides this old nurse who wore white plastic shoes that looked like duck feet was Gin. Gin had a job, and she had promised to do it. I don't want to see him, I told her. I don't want to hear him. Gin is so tall that she had to kneel on the ground to hold my hand in both of hers. This nurse in the duck feet counted *One two, one two* and said things like, *You can do it, you're almost there,* like they do in the movies, but I couldn't and I wasn't.

Hell of a way to spend your birthday, I said to Gin, between the pain, but she just nodded and held me better. The blood and the shit rushed out of me then and I felt the good thing that had been happening in my body that year rush out of me too and I realized that I'd forgotten to tell Gin that I didn't want to smell him either because if anyone brought him within three feet of my nose I would smell what it is like all the way up in my body where there is no sin record, where nobody ever has been or can ever go, and so when the nurse made for me in her white duck feet with my son in her arms, Gin put her eyeballs against my eyeballs and I screamed and I didn't stop screaming until Gin had explained to the nurse and the nurse had finally gotten it through her skull that I was just a dumb whore and nobody's mother.

Gin did her job. I turned away, but I smelled him anyway.

That was my favorite birthday.

. . .

A cry, *Happy Birthday!*, goes up from the crowd, and goes up, and goes up. My eyes are closed and I'm good there, in the space between my mind and my eyelid with someone else's mouth mashed against my mouth. It's Gin's mouth of course. Rachel is in the corner putting candles in the cake and Ray is lighting them. Gin steps back from me and stumbles.

There is singing and Rachel offers the cake up to Gin. She huffs the candles out and flicks her eyes around the bar, hugs Rachel into her armpits. Tex brings me a piece of cake on a white paper napkin and I eat it with my fingers. It's rich and good. Gin is hugging everyone in the room. I see Rachel sitting at the disco-ball end of the bar, wiping her eyes. Then I see her standing outside, looking at her phone. She looks up and watches Gin through the plate-glass window. Rachel watches Gin dance with Wade, watches Gin trip and Wade catch her, watches Gin walk over to the cigarette vending machine and fumble with the plastic around a new pack.

Later, I see Rachel coming out of the bathroom. Then she's standing next to me and leaning against the shiny surface of the bar. Ray hands her a shot of whiskey filled to the brim and she goes down to it, then tips the rest back. She wipes her mouth with the back of her hand, then taps the empty shot glass down.

When you see Gin, Rachel says, tell her I had to go.

You got it, I say.

You know, Rachel says—like she's had this line ready all her life and has been waiting for someone like me to come along so she can say it—you're not good, she says. You're not a good friend.

No one agrees with you more than me, I say. But if you're looking for a friend, you're in the wrong place.

I am, Rachel says. I absolutely am.

She grabs her helmet from a hook underneath the bar. Clang goes the door.

I head for the bathroom. The walls are chalkboard and they're covered with drunk-people thoughts. I read the newest ones while I pee: WHY, MELINDA? E & T 4EVER. I let my head hang down, let the ends of my hair brush the wet floor. Hunched over like that, I look left. Someone has written in small, neat, lawyer print: I THINK I'M IN LOVE WITH GIN.

Gin is still dancing with her assistant manager—arms in the air, eyes closed.

I find Tex outside, leaning against the window.

Tex, I say, and kiss him.

OK, he says. I confess. The name's John.

The sign that says RAY'S HAPPY BIRTHDAY BAR lights his face up with red, and I see how old he is, possibly fifty. I don't want him anymore, but I've been promising all night.

Tracy, he says, in my bed. He takes his eyes from mine then, burying his face between my breasts.

In a house with square shrubs sharp as cubes and a disappointing swing set, my son is ten and it is his birthday, again.

After we have sex, for once, I do not search the ceiling. I

roll over and look at Tex. His hair has come out of his ponytail and spreads over my pillow.

Come on, he says. Tell me something no one at the bar knows. Tell me your birthday.

So I tell him. My birthday is in April. I'm an Aries, the first sign in the zodiac, a natural-born pioneer. I have ideas. For instance, a new, larger disco ball for the bar. For instance, that men and women are not so different, but to really believe that in any way that would matter, I would need to die and start my life all over again. For instance, that Gin signed up that day at the red metal table and then again at the hospital. And who, I'd like to know, when they are lost in the dark, is saint enough to turn away someone who's begging to join them there?

Tracy! Gin hollers, waking me.

Tex/John is gone. I'm in my bra, and though the towels on my windows are keeping the light out, I can feel the heat of the new day.

Gin bangs on my door, not with her fist, I can tell, but with the flat of her palm.

Open up, she says. Please, she says.

Or what? I want to say. I'd like to see her kick the door down. I'd like to hear her walk away.

I let the door swing wide. Gin's suspenders have come unclipped and hang to her ankles like shackles. To my face, she's quiet, sulky as a child.

Make me happy, she says, coming into my room but leaving the door open behind her. It's my birthday.

THE DAN GRAVES SITUATION

Meredith Lovelace was hoping to resolve the Dan Graves situation before lunch. It was Monday, the day she liked to meet her wife, Amy, at the cart on campus for soup and sourdough rolls.

The situation concerned two newly admitted graduate students to the art department at their small-town Pennsylvania state university—both sculptors, both Meredith's advisees. Cara Morris claimed that Dan Graves had shown up on the steps of her apartment building the night before—blotto, talking suicide, and toting a suitcase of letters from his dead dad.

"He told me he wanted to get in his truck and crash it," Cara had said earlier that morning while whipping tissues from the box in Meredith's office. "He told me he wanted to die."

It was not exactly that Meredith thought Cara was lying about the Dan Graves situation. As assistant director of the master of fine arts program, Meredith's job was essentially to answer emails. But in the two months since the new class had arrived, Cara, young and fresh out of undergrad, had emailed more than her fair share—asking to take a sociology course instead of the required graduate arts survey, or urging Meredith to bring in a queer nonbinary Nepalese tile worker who had recently exploded in popularity online as the semester's visiting artist instead of the prize-winning white male welder whose first-class travel from Los Angeles Meredith had been coordinating for three months.

"When I asked Dan Graves to leave, he called me a dyke," Cara had added near the end of their interview. *Dyke,* Meredith typed into the draft window of her email. The cursor disappeared then reappeared. There was no official protocol or online form for this exact situation, as graduate students fell into a weird gray area of responsibility re: the university, but Meredith felt she should make a record of it, for herself, and to defuse Cara's fury.

"Do you hear what I'm saying?" Cara said. She had big breasts and a chain that connected the top cartilage of her left ear to a stud in the lobe. It hung long and shimmering as a stalactite and shook in the air against her bushy hair when she spoke.

"Absolutely," the Director said, leaning back in the flimsy plastic chair he had brought into Meredith's office. "We are taking this very seriously."

Cara looked from the Director to Meredith. Her eyelashes were wet and she wiped her nose with a strangely pink tissue. She seemed to expect something from Meredith that she did not from the Director, perhaps the additional fuzziness of lesbian solidarity. When Meredith and Cara passed each other in the art building's cinderblock stairwells, Cara would smile warmly, then nudge the tip of her chin quickly upward in the kind of micro-nod that lays a claim.

"We are," Meredith said. "We hear you."

When the door closed behind Cara, the Director clapped his hands together. "Those are the magic words," he said. "Just knock on Dan's door and see if he's alive. That's what we did with Ronda last year. Let's hope this goes the other way."

Dan Graves lived in an unhip part of the college town, a residential neighborhood near the woods, in a small stucco house painted mint green. The driveway was short, so in order to park out of the flow of traffic, it was necessary for Meredith to nudge her Volvo station wagon all the way up nose-to-ass against the bumper of Dan Graves's white pickup. The pickup had a single bumper sticker—SAY YA TO THE UP, EH?—and a Michigan license plate, which was clean and perfectly flat. Meredith inspected the truck carefully for signs of an accident, but it was showroom-shiny, possibly brand-new, with a clean black bed-liner. The footwells had been vacuumed so recently that Meredith could still see the overlapping lines of the nozzle, and a stadium cup holding a mountain of quarters was wedged in the middle console. A sensible, admirable thing, that cup. Standing in front of parking meters on campus, Meredith was always rummaging in her pockets, only to turn up dimes, pennies, or an earring of Amy's.

Meredith walked up the stone path and stepped onto Dan Graves's porch. To the right of the front door, a faded American flag hung from two nails. Meredith pushed the button on the storm door with her thumb and pulled the plexiglass toward her. The button wobbled in its socket and clicked halfway but the door did not release. She tried again, pulling harder, and when it still didn't open, she knocked lightly on the storm door with her knuckles. The sound rattled the glass, but didn't penetrate. She waited. Dan Graves did not come. How long was sufficient? A minute? Two? His car was here, after all.

Meredith had met Dan Graves only once before, at the Director's annual lawn party to welcome the new class. He had seemed plodding and straitlaced, not a guy given to dramatics. Meredith remembered him as tall and shy; he had eaten a lot of fried chicken, drank only root beer, and left early. She had made sure to meet him. He was her advisee, after all, but also she liked the work, plain and simple. The images he'd submitted with his application had stuck in Meredith's brain: a deer antler that had grown swollen and infected (in bronze), a large-as-life elk that cowered on its back feet (in bronze), and—Meredith's favorite—a walleye that lay split open and bleeding against a rock (in bronze). It seemed, even in the half-lighting and bad quality of the pictures, that at any moment the fish's eye might blink and its coagulated blood might begin to ooze.

"Oy," one of Meredith's colleagues, a watercolorist, had said during admissions deliberations. "Isn't this the kind of macho-nostalgia that belongs in a place called the Soaring Eagle Lodge?"

But Meredith had praised the work's energy and simplicity, and the Director had backed her up.

. . .

Meredith was halfway back down the stone path when she heard the storm door open.

"It sticks sometimes."

Dan Graves was even thinner than Meredith remembered, and he stood on the porch with his bare feet close together. His eyes were small and set back deeply into his head, which was surprisingly bare for such a young man, the pale skin covered only by a fine translucent fuzz. He wore a red-and-white-checked dress shirt that bore the faint creases of being professionally pressed and folded, and expensive-looking black corduroy pants. He retreated into the foyer of the house as Meredith advanced, but kept his hand against the storm door so that it stayed open.

"I'm not properly dressed," Dan Graves said. "But will you come in?"

To cross the threshold, Meredith had to pass very close to Dan Graves. She was tall for a woman, five-ten on a good day, but she came up only to the top button of Dan Graves's shirt. He smelled of a sporty masculine deodorant, the one that Meredith also wore. He was an attractive man, Meredith observed. Most women would think so.

Dan Graves let the storm door slam. The entryway was carpeted in a thick white shag. Meredith checked her watch. She had twenty minutes if she wanted to catch Amy. On the one hand, it was no big deal, there would be countless weeks left in their life together to eat lunch. On the other, Amy had seemed dark ever since they'd gotten back from visiting her sister and her sister's husband and their twin girls in Philly.

"It's not that I regret we stopped trying," Amy had said at

the kitchen table, the ends of her dark hair brushing the rim of her bowl of rigatoni with sauteed butternut squash. "It was my call, I was the one. It's just that there's always that question, that extra pressure on us maybe, and on our careers. Will we love each other that much more, will our jobs be cool enough, our students sweet enough, our marriage special enough to fill that space, all that time that other people spend on their kids?"

Meredith had taken Amy's many-silver-ringed hand and kissed it. "We will, it will," Meredith had said. When Amy didn't seem satisfied, she'd added, "But I hear you."

"Will you take your shoes off?" Dan Graves said now. "If you don't mind. It's hard work to keep a white carpet clean."

Meredith bent down and unlaced the men's baby blue suede oxfords that Amy had bought her for their anniversary—seventeen years of being together, nine married. Meredith had ogled the shoes from outside the window of the downtown store for a month. On the night Amy gave them to her, Meredith got out of bed to turn on the closet light and hold the shoes in their white tissue paper. They were ridiculous shoes, Meredith saw now, looking at their garish color against Dan Graves's white carpet.

The white carpet continued in every direction. To the right, there was a door—his bedroom, probably—but Dan Graves led Meredith left into the living room.

The big room was empty of furniture, just the white carpet and a raised platform of hardwood that supported a fireplace. In front of the fireplace, a fifties-era green plaid suitcase with gold clasps lay on its side. Across the room were sliding glass doors that opened out onto a wooden deck, and beyond that, a view of the Allegheny Mountains. A small square of sun hovered on the near wall.

Dan Graves rubbed his hands together like he was cold, and looked over at the wooden platform, where there was also a bottle of Old Crow and a squat plastic tumbler. He strode to the platform, gently nudged the bottle and tumbler to the side, then sat down with his back to the fireplace.

"We can sit on this," Dan Graves said. He looked like a grasshopper: all knees.

Meredith did, but left enough space for two of herself to sit between them.

"Dan, do you know why I'm here?"

"I think so," he said. "I got drunk and scared Cara."

"You did," Meredith said. "And you said some things. Things the department is required to take very seriously."

"Damn it." He said it with a pronounced Midwestern accent so that the words came out through his nose—*dee-yam*.

"Cara said you indicated you might be a danger to yourself," Meredith said. "She said you told her you wanted to die."

Dan Graves looked down at his narrow thighs. Meredith could believe almost anything about men but she could never believe their kneecaps, how sharp they were, pointy as bowling pins. With his eyes looking down, everything about Dan Graves's face changed. The lids of his eyes looked pale and veined and there were deep purple shadows around his sockets. The skin of his face was red and raw.

"I don't deny anything," said Dan Graves. When he looked back up at Meredith, his face was neutral again.

"I'm sorry," Meredith said. "I'm very sorry to hear that."

Dan Graves lifted his shoulders to his ears and dropped them. He jiggled his knee, then tapped his bare foot against the carpet.

"I said what I said and I probably meant it at the time. But I'm okay now, Professor Lovelace. You don't have to worry about me. I've slept, I feel a world better."

The wind blew around a few brown leaves that had landed on Dan Graves's deck. The mountains were just starting to turn. It was October. She could go now, Meredith knew. But something about the room tugged at her. The walls were gray and bare. There was no art of any kind here, nor any sign that art was being made.

"How do you like your studio?" Meredith asked. Each graduate student was assigned a small sunny space in a brutalist building on campus.

"Oh, I hate that place," Dan Graves said. "I never go."

He reached for the bottle of whiskey that still sat to the side on the platform. It was a big glass bottle, but it fit neatly in his hand. Dan Graves unscrewed the cap and poured two fingers of whiskey into the tumbler. He brought it to his lips, slurped a few sips, then drained the rest. The bottle was more than half empty. It occurred to Meredith that Dan Graves was very drunk—still, perhaps, or again.

"How about you don't drink any more while I'm here?" Meredith said.

"Alright," Dan Graves said. "That's fair."

A moment passed, then another. Dan Graves leaned down to the suitcase and touched it.

"Would you like to hear a letter from my dad?" he said. "My dad is dead now."

When he said *dad* and *dead,* they came out sounding the same.

Meredith glanced quickly at her watch. Amy's lunch break was half over; Meredith had missed her.

"Alright," Meredith said.

Dan Graves seemed pleased. He slid to the carpet and sat cross-legged. With a snap of his big thumb and middle finger, he released the gold-plated fasteners so that the two halves of the suitcase jumped away from each other. Inside were white envelopes, torn open. He plucked a letter from the suitcase, then held it up with both hands for Meredith to see, like a game show host. His name and address were scrawled across the front in old-timey script.

Dan Graves read out the date, August 17 of the present year. "*Dear Pal,*" he read. "That's what he always called me." Dan Graves looked up at Meredith to see if she was listening. When he saw she was, he reached for the bottle and gave himself a refill. He nestled the bottle in the hole his legs made, then set the tumbler on the platform behind him.

"See?" Dan Graves said. "I didn't drink it."

Meredith said nothing. She was familiar with alcoholics and the fruitlessness of fighting with one.

"*Dear Pal,*" Dan Graves read. "I read that part already."

"Remember the Porkies? Remember when we camped there and we tried to push the tent poles into the ground and how they

wouldn't go in more than an inch? The wind farms around there are getting bigger. Now when I go on my walks, there's geese carcasses everywhere. I can't camp without you. Camping is nothing alone."

"You see?" Dan Graves said. "He loved me."

"Of course," Meredith said. "Of course he did."

Dan Graves looked down at the letter in his hands. "If I could cry, I would cry and I would not stop crying."

"Go ahead," Meredith said. "Go right ahead and cry. It's fine."

"I want to." Dan Graves made a sound in his mouth like a gun cocking. "Hmm," he said. He lifted the glass and drank from it.

Dan Graves read letter after letter aloud to Meredith, pausing after each letter, and sometimes in the middle of a long one, to drink from the tumbler or refill it. The square of light moved slowly across the wall.

"Dear Pal—You caught the walleye with nothing but your hand and then bashed its head against a stone. What a bleeder!"

"Dear Pal—At your aunt's place you built sculptures out of the driftwood that came down the St. Mary and I sat on the porch and forgot you were there. How could I forget? I don't know. I think it was because of the light, how it didn't get dark until very late, 11 maybe, because then the news would come on."

"Dear Pal—What are the grocery stores like there? Can you get a hunting license? How much does one cost? Tell me how much and I'll send you the money."

Dan Graves set down the last letter. "He wrote to me every day I was away from home until last week when he died. That's fifty-seven letters." He scrunched his eyes and made breath-sucking noises. He held the bridge of his nose between his index finger and thumb.

The square of light was weak now, had become distorted. Now that he was crying, Meredith wished he wouldn't. There were a thousand ways to fuck up a child, it seemed, and only time would tell your unique, trademark method. Dan Graves's dad's was being good and then dying.

When Dan Graves was done, he put his open palm to his eyes, gathered the fingers into a duckbill, and shook the tears onto the white carpet.

"I don't know why he asked me about the Porkies. That's what we called the Porcupine Mountains Wilderness, but we haven't been there in, I dunno, fifteen years," Dan Graves said.

"People remember all kinds of things when they're dying," Meredith said.

"Where were you fifteen years ago?" Dan Graves asked.

Meredith smiled. He was a good kid, and curious about her, and she felt sorry for him.

"I was here," she said.

"No," Dan Graves said. "Where *were* you, actually, like in life? I want to know."

Meredith thought. Fifteen years ago, Meredith was twenty-seven and in her last semester as a graduate student in the department. She was still making her art then—collages of human faces from pieces of slate tile and Scotch tape. She made the collages, nearly one a week, in a desperate, hungry fashion that made her forget to eat for hours and then, starving, eat with the fridge door open, sitting on a milk crate. She and Amy lived in a small cottage near Bald Eagle State Forest and far from campus. She wore brown Carhartt overalls almost every day. They carpooled to town and then she told Amy to take the car since Amy was already teaching a rigorous schedule for the English department. Meredith walked everywhere, stopping at coffee shops and parking lots and bars around town to watch people she might want to use for her collages. She had an iPod mini. Touching its smooth and tiny silver face, she listened to the soundtrack of the movie that had not yet been made about the life she had not yet lived. It was a good soundtrack: expansive, unexpected, full of grace and reversals.

These people, she had begun to think that year, looking around the seminar room at the faces of the other graduate students in her cohort—mostly men and a few straight white women who deferred hideously to the men. When her work was critiqued, everyone said her collages were too faithful to life, too descriptive, too pastoral. Alan, as she had called him before he became the Director, was the only one who spoke up for her work, though he did so with one foot in her camp and one foot in the camp of her detractors, as if he were apologizing to them subtextually even as he disagreed. After critique, Meredith often went to a dive bar with him to complain about their colleagues and professors. So pretentious! So bourgeois! So disaffected!

"So true," Alan had said. "But who cares what they think. Soon you'll be living in New York or LA and these guys will just be good stories to tell at dinner parties."

Once, after a particularly brutal critique, Alan had invited Meredith over to the house where he lived with his girlfriend who was a yoga teacher. The girlfriend had paused her work stretching canvases for Alan to go hunt down a book about anger by a Buddhist monk, which she pressed into Meredith's hands. Say your house is on fire, the book said. Would you run down the street after the arsonist demanding to know why he set the blaze? Meredith thought she might. No! the book said. If you did that, all your stuff would burn. Forget the arsonist; all arsonists have their reasons. Run toward your house. Care for your anger, the book suggested. Care for it like a child.

"I was a student in the program, too," Meredith told Dan Graves. "It was hard at times, but also good, and I lived with my wife, but we weren't married yet."

"The girl you loved fifteen years ago. You're married to her now?"

"I am," Meredith said.

"That's good. You really had it together."

"Not really," Meredith said.

"Oh no?" One of Dan Graves's eyelids drooped, then fluttered lightly. "It sounds like you did," he said. "Unless there's something else."

There was something else. She had not ever yelled during her critiques or flipped the seminar table, but she had taken that desire and channeled it into tiny acts of cruelty against people she would never see again, people who did not matter and who she did not believe in—the telephone operator at her bank, the woman who worked the counter at the cupcake store, a stranger who came to buy an old desk she had in storage.

"I was very angry that year," Meredith said.

"I'm angry all the time," Dan Graves said.

"I looked at other women, women who were not my wife."

That year, and if she was being honest, still, Meredith often saw women—at the bars, on the bus, in the coffee shop, even undergraduate students jogging around campus—who she wanted to have sex with. They were all conventionally attractive—thin with big breasts and long hair. Amy was pretty, no doubt about it, but she did not look like these women. Alan's girlfriend did, and when Meredith returned the book on Buddhism to her, they had had a moment, or so Meredith had thought, an opening where she could have seduced the woman, almost had, but didn't. Then, later that year, in a used-book store, Meredith had opened a Christian-y book and seen that the previous owner had underlined a short passage: *There is the thief. There is the liar. There is the man whose wife is not enough for him, who cannot be happy until he possesses every woman who walks the earth.*

"I want women so much," Dan Graves said. "I think"—he paused—"that's what happened with Cara."

"Meaning?" Meredith asked.

"I told her that she was pretty. So pretty. And she told me she was gay. And I told her she couldn't be gay because I wanted her."

"Not cool," Meredith said. "Very not cool."

"I know," Dan Graves said. "But I couldn't help it."

Dan Graves drank from his glass. The square of sun was gone.

"We could go outside," Dan Graves said. "It's a nice afternoon." When he got up and opened the glass doors and went out to stand on the deck, Meredith followed. The chill came through the fabric of her wool sweater and button-down and landed on her skin.

The smell of the woods reminded her again of the little cabin she and Amy had lived in and the trips they'd taken, spending the night with nothing but a sleeping bag and some packets of ramen.

"I'd like to go camping," Meredith said.

"You camp?" Dan Graves laughed. "You don't, not really."

For a moment, Meredith believed him, believed that he could tell her about herself somehow, that he saw her story in its completeness and was wise. She had always been porous in this way, and prone to hoping.

But then Dan Graves leaned over onto the deck's wooden railing, hocked back a great confluence of saliva, and spit it out. His spit landed in some low shrubs. He wiped his chin with his hand.

"I do camp," Meredith said. "What makes you think I don't?"

"You're a city girl. I could tell by your shoes. Pop quiz: What's the best way to build a fire?"

Dan Graves had his arms crossed over his chest. He was puffed up now, triumphant, happy, feeling no pain.

"Cara said you called her a dyke. At her house, when she asked you to leave."

Dan Graves blinked his blond eyelashes. "I don't remember," he said. "But if Cara says I did, then I did. Cara's not a liar."

Stop, Meredith could have said to him. Stop now. Stop today. But she said nothing.

Dan Graves yawned a big, loud yawn, then hugged himself with his huge hands. The light had changed and the woods, which belonged to Dan Graves and his dead dad, were dark beyond the deck.

Meredith turned to look at the living room and the open suitcase through the sliding doors. Dan Graves would not remember anything tomorrow. Even if he did, who would believe him now, discredited as he was—a drunk, a homophobe?

Dan Graves finished what was left in his glass. "Brrrrrr," he groaned loudly, then leaned against the railing of the deck, holding on with his hands. His eyes closed, and his head drooped for several minutes. Then he straightened up and was awake again. "I'm cold," he slurred.

Meredith's chest felt energized, her legs spry. She went back inside the house. She gathered the letters and their empty envelopes and returned them to the green suitcase, then lifted the suitcase up onto the wooden platform. She opened a letter so that it lay flat, then rolled it the long way into a thin tube. She stood before the fireplace, removed its screen, and balanced the rolled letter between the andirons.

Dan Graves filled the doorway, his body backlit.

"Hey," Dan Graves said. His eyes were on her, but he had that other look about him.

Letter by letter, layer by layer, the log cabin began to take shape.

"I'm so cold," Dan Graves said again.

"I know it," Meredith said. I'm building you a fire.

BEAUTY

For Jonathan Franzen

It begins when she comments on one of my videos.

Wow, writes LouiseGeez2012. *You're beautiful.*

Hahahaha, I reply right away, then snap the laptop shut.

That night, for the first time in years, I feel beautiful in the conventional sense of the word—pleasing to the eye. I get gloriously high, eat a Red Baron frozen pepperoni pizza, find the half-used bottle of expensive lotion, a hotel exclusive collab left over from my previous life, and warm it between my palms, working it into the pale winter skin between the hairs of my calves with just the tips of my index and middle fingers.

I open the sliding glass door and step naked onto the grass, which is crunchy with frost. The sensation on my feet is surprising but not uninteresting. Skin! That protective covering. In contrast to other body parts, my skin is the same now that I am fat as it was when I was thin. There are birds in the tree line; I can hear them sputtering and hopping as the cold air rushes into my throat, my armpits, my belly button. The moon is the slightest sliver like someone painted a coin black but forgot the edge.

. . .

I live in a valley surrounded by mountains on all sides, which creates a natural dead zone away from the world, a quiet zone, if you will. I will. Wi-Fi and cell signals get in, but very slowly, and if it rains, not at all. I chose this location after I read an article lamenting the near impossibility of high-speed internet in Pennsylvania's most rural areas. The article had a color-coded map showing the average connectivity speeds in each zip code and nowhere was there a bigger swath of white—speeds so low it said NO RESULTS when I hovered my mouse—than here. The closest state park is called Worlds End.

It takes a long time, sometimes an entire day, to upload one twenty-seven-minute video of Terrance, my clown fish, or one sixteen-minute video of me contouring my face. Terrance is missing a fin. He came like that from the exotic-fish store. He's special, the clerk said. He was abused as a child. He has lived a long time but could live much longer.

The idea now is: play. I want to see what happens when I point my phone camera at something, when my face changes shape. I am patient. As the videos upload, I open the bottles of fish food very slowly, pushing down and turning at the same time, or else I run a very hot bath and empty in my most luxurious essential oils drop by drop. If I am sprinkling a flake of food into Terrance's tank, I wait for him to eat it and turn back to me with love in his eyes before letting another flake fall.

. . .

In the morning, she's gone a bit overboard.

Do you have more videos? she's commented again, on a video of me contouring my face to look like the drag queen Divine. *I've watched all 136 of them and there don't seem to be any more. I looked for hours but nothing.*

I stare into the computer, through the black text on the white background of YouTube, and into the solid stuff of the machine. Yesterday I had twelve subscribers; today I have thirteen.

I go about my day. I take my time combing my hair in the sun and make a video of it, using a very small comb and working section by section. I work the knots through.

Back at the computer, she's commented once more: *Please, Marion. Please let me know.*

What you see is what I have, I reply to her comment. *It takes me time. I am very busy.*

Within minutes, her reply: *I can pay.*

I go outside and grill a hamburger, contemplating this offer. On the one hand, I am nearing the last of my Lavender money and there is that hole in the bathroom wall through which carpenter bees have been entering and pulverizing the wood. On the other hand, once you sell someone your face, it splinters off from your head. If too many of your faces are circulating independent of your body, it can be very destabilizing. One can become destabilized. The last time I was presented with this choice, I preferred instead to disassemble my whole life, piece by piece.

. . .

She sends me money using the same username on a different app. We do not agree on a specific price, but the first payment arrives and it is five hundred dollars. To represent the reason for the money visually, she chooses cartoon fish. We message through the private app that allows you to text freely with everyone in the world except China, which has its own app.

Slow down, big spender. That's a lot of fish.

It's ok. My dad owns the only carpet store for three counties. We are rich. He had a good year last year and expects a record-breaking quarter.

You are, what, in high school, Louise?

I say this as a joke based on her profile picture, which is consistent across all the apps—a picture of the boy child celebrity who swoops his hair like a woman.

It's Lou. Middle school. But I'm very mature. My grandmother started a weird school in the woods near Lancaster that teaches people about their bodies. She taught me about exploitation and how America actually lost the Vietnam War and that Eleanor Roosevelt was a lesbian.

Is that for sure? I mean, is it proven?

She sends a shrug emoji, a white man with dark brown hair in a blue sweater turning both of his palms to the sky.

What is proof?

After that first conversation, it is a beautiful afternoon—clear and cold. The sun touches every surface of my one-room house, warming the scratchy multicolored blankets on my bed and casting rainbows on the surface of Terrance's tank. It is a perfect afternoon to engage in my Sex Routine, so I engage in it. First I shower, making sure to wash the crevices between the flesh of my upper pussy area and thighs, between my ass cheeks, and underneath my breasts with a tea tree–based soap to prevent the painful red splotches that sometimes bloom there. Next, I crank the wooden ceiling fan to its swiftest speed, lie down on the carpet on my largest bath towel, and let myself air-dry. Once I am seventy-five to eighty percent dry, I begin to masturbate.

I always picture the same woman for my Sex Routine,

though I can never decide on her size or race. Sometimes she is larger and sometimes she is smaller, sometimes she is as porcelain pale as an actress in a Regency period drama and sometimes she is the dark brown of a piece of black walnut furniture, but all the other details remain consistent. I picture a woman with a large ass and a soft stomach and soft upper arms. I picture her on her knees straddling someone—me possibly, or a man.

Her breasts are the main attraction, large but in a particular way, fibrous, with a certain structural integrity. The kind of breasts that would offer robust side boob and also underboob if one put them in a small triangle bikini that covered only the nipples and areolas. Actually, the areolas are the most important part. I always imagine breasts with very large areolas, heavy and pendulous and a little tubular.

In my mind's eye, I suck my dream woman's breasts for a long time, licking and then rubbing my nose in my own saliva until she is very aroused. In real life, the fan is whipping overhead and my hand is whipping between my legs and a few seconds before I come I have to decide, once and for all, if I am the person doing the licking or if I am the person being licked, as my dream woman does bear a striking resemblance to me. I tend to alternate, choosing both roles in different moments and moods. Today I choose licked.

Tell me about your school.

You don't want to hear.

You won't bore me.

There's nothing boring about it. It's terrifying, straight terror, terror all day. When I don't feel afraid, I don't feel anything.

Yes. I think I remember that.

There is one good thing. I have a bag of different colored erasers I can zip open and closed. The zipper is very satisfying.

What about your parents?

They're ok.

Mysterious.

My dad has a big family and my mom has a small one. My dad took her into his. They love each other. They love me. Inside this house, I'm good. But outside it.

Hmm.

I dress like a boy. But I'm not a boy.

I noticed. Do you wear hats?

Hats?

Hats.

Yeah, I have an Eagles hat I like.
I like the color green. My dad has
his brothers over on Sundays and
they let me sit and watch and
give me chips.

What kind of chips?

Sour cream and onion.

Mmm.

A thousand more dollars appear in my bank account.

I have not forgotten her opening remark, that she finds me beautiful. It sits there in the back of my mind, like a sofa I am deliberately not lying on. In real life, I don't have a sofa, just a black faux leather desk chair where I sit when I am using the computer. If anything, there are too many sofas in this town. I have seen them at the Goodwill, overstuffed sofas in corduroy and denim, soft and comfortable places to rest. I worry that if I got one and brought it home and lay down on it, I might never get up again.

Some years ago, I worked enough for a lifetime. Every day just after sunrise, I would take a form of transportation in which a car of people is pulled along a set of tracks by an electrical wire, first aboveground in the flow of traffic, and then below it. If a car was double-parked and dallying, we could wait thirty minutes hanging there. I would emerge like a mole into daylight, aka the city of Philadelphia, where I would make my way to the main station and board a train to the suburbs, disembarking near the entrance to a Catholic party university and then walking twenty minutes on a posh two-lane road with no shoulder to Jenn's parents' house.

I'd met Jenn, plus our third, Beatrice, at that university—not technically but narratively. We'd met many times before at Penn track practice, but it was there, as juniors at an exhibition meet when it rained, that we first really spoke. Distance runners, all three of us. This was 2012, so we had phones and were on them, but not in the way people are on them now.

Your hair, Jenn said to me as we sat, damp on the squeaky gym floor, eating granola bars. She was tall, with shins like candlepins—cankles, she called them—splayed out in front of her. She made a gesture around her head suggesting frizz and handed me a stretchy purple headband.

I put it on.

Beatrice leaned over. She had the kind of freckles across her nose that women now apply with an eyeliner pen.

Got another? Beatrice asked Jenn.

She did, also purple.

Drunk on Spruce Street, I lost the headband soon after, but it didn't matter. By then we were pregaming and brunching and moving into a triple together for our senior year. After graduation, we all took jobs in various soft-skilled and public-relations-adjacent fields until Jenn had the idea to start Lavender, a direct-to-consumer beauty brand aimed at female athletes, and raised a bunch of money from her parents' rich friends. We produced only four products: a tinted sunscreen, a sweatproof blush stick, a waterproof mascara, and a pigmented lip balm with SPF.

In the beginning, of course, we produced nothing, only drawings and social media posts. As we sat around the marble island at Jenn's parents' house, Jenn would do this thing where she would test for fatness by taking her thumb and middle finger and encircling her wrist. If her fingers touched, she was in a good mood—bopping all over the zebra-skin rug with her pen tapping against her notepad; if they didn't, she'd guzzle MiraLAX and spend the rest of the afternoon texting us from the bathroom.

But over time and fueled by sushi and ramen packets and salads—so many salads, so much quinoa, so many sweet potatoes, so many black beans (*Protein,* Jenn would intone, *you need to up your protein intake!*)—we did produce things. Beatrice and I produced farts and fart jokes and Jenn produced one thousand tiny poops. Our capitalistic output was packaged in organic purple cotton bags and every purchase came with a free gift of a light purple athletic headband that Beatrice and I designed together, she researching and actualizing the special hair-gripping technology, and I choosing the fabric and the exact shade of lavender from thousands of samples. Jenn was the brain, Beatrice was the grind, and I was the eyes.

Eventually, as Lavender prospered, we moved our headquarters and rented a glass cube inside a coworking space in Manhattan. All day long Jenn and I drank seltzer from the bottomless seltzer dispenser and eyed each other over imitation-crystal goblets. It's difficult to remember much about that period because I was so hungry. Beatrice claimed a fast metabolism and natural thinness, and there may have been some truth to this as I did thrice see her consume French fries dipped in a mixture of ketchup and mayonnaise, but Jenn and I were both hormonally imbalanced and predisposed to pudge. Since the hours previously spent running had been replaced with working, dieting and purging were constant activities, items on the daily agenda: ideate, communicate, develop, shit, test, revise, starve. I remember an oatmeal raisin cookie split four ways with a visiting plastics vendor rep. I remember Jenn bringing a pear up to her teeth and then putting it back in the bowl with enormous tenderness. After she walked away, I picked up the pear, put my teeth where hers had been, and bit down.

We began to be photographed. Constantly. The three of us. The Lavender Girls, they called us. No one—least of all me—wanted to be on either side, all of us jostling for the middle spot. In the photo shoot ahead of our first official product launch, I snagged the middle by ignoring a call that Jenn then had to take, but it didn't matter. When we got the pictures back, it was like I was on a different scale, or like someone had zoomed in on me but left the two of them alone. We made a strange shape—they the two sides of a narrow tunnel and I the tunnel's huge opening.

Then Lavender entered the process for acquisition by a Silicon Valley pharmaceutical company, and the feedback was immediate and direct. There was no dancing, there was no beating, there was only the bush and the bush was my body: *What can be done about Marion's weight?* was the way they put it in person. In (confidential) writing, I was a line item—*improve Marion's appearance to be more befitting of an ambassador for a fitness brand*—along with other things such as *update cotton vendors* and *implement 3.0 cash flow system.*

To finalize the deal, we met in our bizarrely small conference room. My chair scraped the glass wall when I leaned back.

By the end of the meeting, I had a cash offer—very generous.

I'm sorry, Jenn said afterward, in the hallway.

So sorry, Beatrice said. That was— She paused. That was fucked-up.

I looked at Jenn. Though five years had passed, she looked exactly the same as the day I'd met her, that same girl from college. Her bangs, her wrists, her cankles—which she usually concealed in wide-legged denim but which that day were on full display below her short leather skirt.

You could run, Jenn said. That's what I do. At night, late like midnight, when the city's quiet. I listen to heavy metal. Weird, I know, but it helps.

Helps with what? I asked.

Everything, she said.

Jenn and Beatrice stayed. Almost immediately, Jenn accelerated, Beatrice procreated, and I relocated. My body stretched, and quickly.

Lou and I are talking again, late at night, through the app. Money has been arriving steadily in my account each week.

Why the fish?

I was born on an island between Delaware and Maryland. A small island. You could cross it in an afternoon.

But why the fish videos?

Have you ever felt the need to document something? When you see something almost too amazing to be real and it feels like a crime to keep it to yourself? Like if people saw this and knew it existed . . . It's hard to explain.

I think I know what you mean. Sometimes when I see my dad hug each of his brothers on their way out the door, it feels like that. I sometimes think, wow. If people could see this they would feel— I don't know. Different. Better.

That's nice. But I have long ago given up the hope that the things I do will make people feel better. Those ideas have left me. I watched them go.

Then why?

Sometimes it just feels good to watch something doing exactly what it is made to do, to watch something being beautiful.

I know. That's why I watched you.

—

Are you there?

Mmm hmm.

??

How did you find me anyway?

I'm fat too. I googled "how to make my face look thinner" and that led me to one of your makeup videos.

Haha. That was a fun one.

I like when you said "my blob . . . er, my face." It took me a minute to realize that the contour lines you were drawing on your face were just for fun, not actually for thinness. It was a surprise. I like surprises.

Yeah, that's what my face feels like sometimes.

Totally! You made me laugh. I hadn't laughed in a long time.

No?

No.

Hmm, that's too bad. I laugh a lot. I laugh every day even though I live by myself. That's another reason I have the fish. To laugh. But don't get me wrong, you don't have to be funny. You don't have to be a funny fat person. You can be a sad fat person if you want.

Thanks 😭.

Aw, honey.

—

You there?

Mmm hmm.

BEAUTY

Whatcha doing?

Watching the fish. You?

Watching you.

Creepy.

Sorry. The one where you're brushing your hair. I don't get that one. It's so different from the rest.

Who said I had to stay the same?

That's true. I hate when people don't let me change. Last year my favorite color was green. This year it's yellow.

Good choice.

Thanks. But my mom keeps buying me green shirts. Green shoes.

She's just trying to love you.

Don't do that.

Do what?

Don't try to teach me things. Don't talk down to me like you are the adult and I am the child.

But I am the adult and you are
the child.

Now that I am flush with cash, I buy three bottles of the makeup I use for my videos instead of one. As a child, I did school theater and became a sort of specialist in stage makeup, the idea being: impactful, even from fifty feet away. This requires applying an amount of product that people find alarming. I make a video in which I cut the end of the makeup tube off and drip it onto my face like paint. I rub the foundation into my skin with all the fingertips of both hands, getting some in my hair.

This attracts attention online, though not for the right reasons.

What a waste, someone comments.

No, I reply, the first time I have done so publicly. *Nothing is wasted.*

You there?

Mmm hmm.

What are you doing?

Cutting a pair of pants into jean
shorts. You?

Dunno. Sad.

Why? Bad day at school?

Yeah.

What happened?

Nothing. That's the point. I think I might be bored. I'm realizing that when I get bored, when my mind has nothing to do, I get mean.

Yeah I do that too.

Yeah?

Yeah.

Does it get better when you grow up?

No.

I make a video in which I use makeup on butternut squashes, slathering their bulbous sides.

Again, people are concerned.

What is the point of this? one person comments. *Why would you waste makeup on a vegetable?*

I am playing, I reply. *With me, nothing is ever wasted.*

I try a baseball next, then a baseball cap, pressing the wet brush and tacky contour stick again and again to the thick canvas fabric until it takes.

You there?

hold on

??

OK. Sorry I am at the vet with Terrance.

!! Is he ok?

Don't know yet. Waiting to hear.

I'm so sorry. What happened?

I don't know. Just came home from the grocery store and he was belly up. Breathing but not well. So confusing because I just changed the filter and all his rocks. Oh god.

What?

Maybe I fucked it up. Maybe I killed him.

You didn't.

Are you sure?

No.

Thanks for that.

Sorry, just being honest.

No I mean it, thank you.

For what?

For telling the truth. Nobody does that.

I know. My parents are all like, "you're not fat, you're just big boned." And I'm like, all bones are the same size.

—

Hey you there?

Yeah.

How's Terrance?

He's alive. He looks weird but he's alive and he's swimming.

WOW. I prayed for him.

In response to a comment on one of my videos that I am "tricking" people by contouring my double chin and with my general use of light and shadow, I make a video in which I contour abdominal muscles onto my fat stomach. I drip foundation onto my stomach, using a whole tube in one go, and shake setting powder so liberally that the top comes off and powder falls on my bare thigh. I scoop my brush against my skin to pick up the product and keep going. A well-known makeup artist to the gay stars leaves a comment: *This is WILD, you are a WILD woman.*

—

Hi hello I have great news!

???

I made a new friend!

At school? How is that possible
in March?

Lol I know. She's in my grade but
I didn't know her.

I repeat. How is that possible?

My school is huge, remember?
I remember seeing her in history
maybe once. She said she usually
sits outside for lunch under the tree
by herself. But she changed. Before
she wore flannel. Now she wears
corsets. We're the same size. We
could share clothes if I, ya know,
wanted to wear girlie things.

A fatty in a corset? Score.

I know. The other kids won't know
what hit them. I had a dream
about her. It's so weird but it's
true. I dreamed she came to my
grandmother's school with me
but that we were the teachers. I

dreamed we taught adults how to
smell and hear and taste and touch.

!

Yeah.

—

You there?

I'm here. Terrance is swimming
again. He's swimming these
circles. He looks so happy.

I turn my video of contouring abs onto a fat stomach into a series, buying additional shades of foundation to make the muscles even more lifelike. Then I do an opposite video where, using the same techniques, I add fat rolls to places where I have none—my calves, my ankles, my forearms.

This video, someone comments, *is what is wrong with America today.*

OMG you'll never guess what
Leah did today.

Took her top off? Cursed out a
teacher?

No! Wow sometimes you'd think
you're the thirteen year old and
I'm the adult.

Well.

She made me a fortune teller. Out
of paper, where you put your
hands into it and open and close
your hands and pick a number
and then a letter. I got the coolest
fortune. She told me I would
travel across the United States
alone in a pickup truck.

Be careful what you wish for.

What does that mean?

It means you have a family you
love who loves you.

Don't go being in a hurry to
leave them.

A bird in the bush is worth two
in the hand, etc. Don't count
your chicks before they hatch.

??

!!

I don't really want to be alone
though. I like where I live.

Atta boy.

BEAUTY

—

You there

<>

I don't know what that means.

{}

OK I'm going to assume you're there. Sorry about the money, my grandma is being a bitch.

It's OK.

I'll get it to you soon. I had another dream about Leah. And you were there too!

You dream a lot.

I know, it's the antidepressants I'm on.

☹

It's all good. I love being medicated. I love dreaming. We were on motorcycles this time. You were on a big one, like a hog. And Leah and I were behind you, on small ones, like scooters. We were shooting people, just murdering everyone. Bodies everywhere.

Whoa.

Do you think that's bad? Do you think that's something I shouldn't dream? Do you think that means I really want to murder people?

—

Did you fall asleep? The thing about it was, we were only copying you. You were the one doing the murdering. We were just following orders.

I return to focusing only on my face. Using my now signature pouring and slathering technique, I do a video where I make my face into the face of Ursula the Sea Witch complete with even more chins than I actually have. Someone posts the video to TikTok, where it racks up nearly a million views over the course of three days. I spend those days driving back and forth to the Walmart parking lot to use their Wi-Fi so I can watch myself get exalted, condemned, and defended.

SMDH, you should be ashamed. What a human pile of garbage.

Queen! Bow down!

This is why you don't have a boyfriend.

What is wrong with you? someone comments, to which someone else comments, *What is wrong with YOU that you need to police this woman's joy?*

Crying. Sobbing. Throwing up.

I'm living for this content. Before I was dead, but now I have been brought back to life.

I buy a premade chicken Caesar wrap from Walmart and sleep that night in my car. Lou has messaged seven times but I don't open the app. No one else but her can link the me in this car to the me in the video, and right now I don't want to be linked.

When I wake in the morning, my back is sore and my teeth are fuzzy and someone in the comments has posted a link to my YouTube channel, where the video also goes viral.

Say goodbye, I message Lou without reading what's come before. *I'm deleting all my videos.*

Wait wait wait, Lou says. *Wait until I can download them and keep them.*

For what?

Posterity.

Hahaha, I say.

I do not wait. I delete my YouTube account.

The next day marks two weeks without a payment from Lou. Soon they stop altogether.

> *Hey, are you OK? I'm starting to*
> *get the feeling you don't want to*
> *talk to me anymore.*

Just tired. It's winter. I'm wintering.

I really need to ask you something. In the comments on the video, someone posted a link to an old news article. It says you were a part of this skincare company called Lavender? I can't believe the way you used to look then, like a thin Barbie automaton. I can't believe those girls in all those photos were your friends.

They weren't my friends.

They obviously were though. There's like a thousand pictures of you and them laughing and drinking lattes and holding exercise equipment. Like you were a totally different person.

I thought I was allowed to change.

You are. But like, it's just so drastic. It feels so unlike you.

You mean unlike the me you like. They were my teachers.

What does that mean?

It means they taught me how to wrap my ponytail with pieces of my own hair. They taught me good angles from bad. So now when I am using all these bad angles I'm doing it on purpose.

OK. I think I'm just getting used to the idea of how much you've changed.

I want to change. But have I?

Duh of course you have!

You're not perpetuating anymore. You're refusing.

—

Are you there?

OK. Good night then.

I make a video for no one but me. The video is just on my phone, I upload it nowhere, I show it to no one. In the video, I record myself doing my Sex Routine but it is not a sex video. My Sex Routine takes up the first seventeen minutes, but after that, it is just a video of a fat white woman lying on the floor on top of a bath towel, watching the overhead fan, then flexing her toes, then crying. After the crying, she opens her eyes. She breathes very fast and then less fast, and then slow. Her eyebrows flutter from the oxytocin—the bonding hormone, they call it—and then she is asleep. If it is good enough for Andy Warhol, then it is good enough for her. I watch, for thirty-seven more minutes, as she snores, turns over, at one point throwing her arm hard against the floor and at another bringing her hands together and snuggling them between her breasts like a book or in prayer.

Wow, I can't believe you're really doing this. You're just going to pretend I don't exist now. That really sucks.

—

Hey, I believe this is what the kids call ghosting. You just all of a sudden stop responding? That is so not cool.

—

You think you're so special? Well you're not. There's a hundred cool fat chicks on the internet doing exactly what you're doing but better. They have real cameras and real light setups and are making real commentary about what it means to be a woman and fat in this world and they aren't secretly also toxic diet culture influencers. They have hope. They are inspiring. They don't have weird fish. What is up with that anyway? What is really and truly up with that?

—

Are you there? I know you're there. I can see you're reading these messages. You should turn off read receipts but you probably don't even know how to do that because you're old.

I am here. The problem is that I used to have a body that looked the same, barring race and breast size, as sixty-seven other girls ages eighteen to twenty-one. We would run in a pack around and around Penn's outdoor track, which looks, from the outside, a lot like Rome's Colosseum.

Now I have Terrance and my house and a body that looks the same as people who walk the woods, who drive pickup trucks, who scan my frozen pizzas at Walmart. No one can convince me that the body I had before and the body I have now are not characters in totally different stories.

To try to convince myself, I make a video that is a collage

of myself, in photos, over the years. I start with pictures of myself as a child. Marion as Spider #3 in *James and the Giant Peach.* Marion as Fantine in *Les Misérables,* that pitiful creature who sings "I Dreamed a Dream," about how she had a dream her life would be so different from this hell she is living.

It is not that I am in hell, or if I am, it is the most beautiful hell. Terrance is thriving, swimming around and through his rocks. There are the birds, and the foxes, and even a black bear who flirts with me, overturning my trash cans. My freezer is full of ice cream and also some frozen chili I made the other day, and my fridge is full of pears. But I am in Jenn's hell, and Beatrice's too, and that of the Marion I was when I knew them. And there is something in that, something that is big enough to break your brain. But what? Every time I almost grasp it, it skitters away.

I add "I Dreamed a Dream" as the background song for my video and then take some pictures of me as I am now, of my side rolls and the flesh between my thighs and my double chin. I add them to the end of the video. I do not click "post." I click "save."

Are you there?

—

I just want you to know that you
have broken my heart.

—

This is the most painful betrayal that has ever happened to me, the most painful thing of my whole life.

I can't sleep, I can't eat. My whole sense of who is good and who is bad, who is worth trusting in this world and who is not is broken now.

Leah is worried about me and she never worries. My parents are worried.

—

I just want you to know what you did to me. I want you to know that I will never, not as long as I live, forgive you. Never. Ever. Ever.

MAMA

My daughter's new girlfriend, Cara, is big. Big mouth, big breasts, a tuft of hair so curly it looks permed. My daughter, Beth, has one girlfriend already, the pint-sized Tomboy who drops by every Easter and Christmas.

Mark my words, says Donna from black-belt class, looking over my shoulder at the picture on my phone as we change into our uniforms. This will end in a clusterfuck. No one can have their cake and eat it too.

There's no cake eating, I say, they all know about each other and what they've signed up for. Very modern. Not so different from when you were going out with that postal worker while driving loops around the harbor late at night with a student of philosophy, mmm?

Well, Donna says, folding her capris into the locker's highest shelf.

On the mats, I'm paired with a ponytailed man who goes down easy with a swift kick to the rump. He looks at the ceiling. I look at him. For I also have questions. I am only human. Two girlfriends! What does one person do with so much love?

. . .

Beth calls while I am drinking coffee to say they and Cara will leave Philadelphia after work, then drive south to us through Friday night traffic. They sound breathless, and I can see them on the strange exercise bike they bought—basically a giant fan with pedals. Despite making real money as a doctor of lungs, Beth lives with the Tomboy in a house that has no blinds or real furniture save this bike. I think Beth likes to create harsh conditions so that they can be proud of having overcome them.

Can we go to Chincoteague? Beth asks me, panting. Cara really wants to see ponies, they say, and I need to make it up to her.

What "it"? I say, but they are already off the line.

The dogs stand on the couch, white fluffy twins, watching out the window for Beth's boxy sedan.

A watched pot never boils, I tell them.

That's not real, Mike says, ever the lawyer. It's just a thing to say.

I reach for my practice sword on the kitchen island, wave it between Mike's face and the television, where men are sporting against a green background.

Careful, I say.

Cara beats Beth to the mudroom door and comes in first. She gives me a tight hug, then rests her wide-jeaned butt atop the washing machine. She wears a button-down shirt that looks too soft and rounded to be for business. If I didn't know better, I would think: pajamas. Earrings that hang down but don't match. I like her already.

Beth appears, loaded down with gear. They look like an eight-year-old boy in a blazer, but more underslept. They rub their eyes with the tips of their fingers. Their hair has gone gray above both ears, which gives them a distinguished look. They are thirty-four. When they move to hug me, the ring of keys on their pants makes a clanking sound against the aluminum travel mug clipped to their backpack. They hug me a long time.

Mama, they say.

I'm parched! cries Cara, shooting Beth a look.

I get it, the AC in Beth's car is broken, has been broken. The Tomboy and I have long since given up nagging Beth to get it fixed. But in the context of this new girlfriend, everything seems possible again.

Oh for God's sake, I say to Beth, I'm calling my guy, he can take care of it tomorrow.

And to my great surprise Beth just flops their shoulders. Okay, they say.

Beth and Cara have already eaten sweet potato burritos out of Tupperware in the car, but they want to drink. We sit at the round kitchen table sipping small amounts of whiskey from large plastic tumblers filled with ice. Mike sits in the living room with his back to us. The brown recliner's springs groan every time he reaches for the can on the carpet.

I've always wanted to come to the Eastern Shore, Cara

says to me. Ever since I was a little girl and I read that book about Misty, this pony who roams Chincoteague. She was wild and free and ate sea plants and took no shit. She could kill any of the other ponies no problem.

That's like my mama, Beth says, tipping their cup in my direction.

Oh yeah? Cara takes her own face in her hands, elbows on the table, and wiggles her weight side to side in the wood chair, making it creak, like a round bird in a nest, brooding. She is soft at the tops of her arms and in the middle where her shirt is tighter, where Beth and the Tomboy and I are hard. Her shirt is definitely a pajama top.

Yeah, Beth says. Mama's a black belt now, can take down anyone in her class, even the men. If I was a strange man, I would think twice about messing with her.

I have always wanted to fight, Cara says. I have always had the fight inside me. The world has just never given me a chance to express it.

Lucky you, Beth says.

Don't listen to them, I say, they're a bad example.

I used to get into fights, says Beth.

Understatement of the century, I say. Then, remembering, I add, Punchy cake, punchy cake, punch me in the face.

My guy friends in high school, Beth explains. We used to say that to each other. Then, in college, I walked around campus at night, drunk, just saying it until someone did.

And then she'd call me and cry, I say.

They, Beth corrects. And I never cried.

. . .

Mike is already asleep but I turn my bedside light on anyway. I can hear Beth and Cara down the hall in the guest room talking, their feet moving over the carpet, then nothing.

Mike turns his body to me and starts asking questions.

Joan, he says, what would happen if we bought the Tip Top Diner? Why does salt melt snow? What do you think of the president's face?

This is the part of their father that Beth never sees. These questions progress to other questions.

What if I put my hand here? Mike says.

My hair is trapped underneath my back. My feet itch.

Don't do that, I say.

When I get up to get a glass of water, the guest room is silent but there is a bar of light at the bottom of the door. My kid is on their knees in there, I think, taking the zipper of Cara's jeans into their mouth.

Mike thinks this is not normal, that there are things no parent should know about their child. TMI, he once heard a father say on television—too much information. I know that sometimes, in the right mood and the right weather, Beth enjoys a riding crop applied to their ass, just so. I know what it feels like to have a woman's whole hand inserted into you and then turned.

Like being deflated, Beth once told me.

In a good way?

In a good way.

Also what it feels like to take a human lung in your hands

and deflate it. A lung is like any other thing, they told me. Capable of dying.

I think we parents know these things anyway, so it's coy and false to pretend. For example, I knew it the moment Beth's sex light flicked on, the moment they became aware that they had a body with its own directives, and that other people did too.

It was Saint Patrick's Day, '95 or '96. Beth was maybe ten, we still lived in Baltimore, only came here to the shore on vacation. Upstairs, Mike and the family were taking their time getting hammered. Mike's brother Todd had a sweet tooth and liked to drop shot glasses of sticky sweet Baileys into glasses of Guinness. He liked the patterns the milky stuff made in the dark beer but he always waited too long to drink, hemming and hawing until it curdled.

Todd brought his kids, four boys and one girl. She was small but she was older than Beth. The boys sat on the checkerboard kitchen floor pressing buttons on game consoles with their thumbs while Beth and the girl were downstairs watching a movie. Something set in biblical times. The basement door was open, and up the stairs came the sounds of horse hooves and men being impaled by jousting lances. But when I came back for more ice, it was quiet down there, just static, like they had ejected the tape or been done a long time. After that, Beth's bedroom door was always closed and their forkfuls of mashed potatoes lingered in the air a full minute before meeting their mouth.

Another time I watched out the kitchen window as Beth and their guy friends from high school ran across our lawn toward the trees. Through the trees was a parking lot and then the school. They were wild, our kids, but in a tight container. Most of the boys stood at the tree line, throwing water bottles of booze up into the branches for the last boy, perched there, to catch. Beth walked slowly over the grass. They were drunk. I could see it in the way their arms hung slack at their sides and in the way they kept pushing their greasy hair out of their eyes with their hands. And then a girl came up behind Beth. Beth stopped and turned toward the girl. Beth raised their face. They waited a long time to be kissed. I knew then that there is something in my child that likes to submit, that savors standing still while someone moves in upon them.

In the morning, I'm up early with the dogs. Mike likes to lie in bed a long time and think. The dogs roll and bite each other through my legs as I walk them down the street and back, and I think, Alright, okay, this is living. They settle below the dryer as it rumbles. Beth comes in, mashing a bowl of cereal.

Where's Cara? I say.

She works nights answering crisis calls, Beth says. She dropped out of grad school last year and is still figuring out her life. She'll be asleep a long time.

Beth talks to me about their patients—a man who waited two years to get a lung transplant only to immediately go skydiving and come back with a collapsed lung.

Some people never learn, they say. Conversely, they tell me about a woman who installed wildly expensive air filters throughout her house whose lungs are turning scarred and stiff at a rate which defies all science.

Her body is just attacking itself, Beth says. We've tried everything. We can't stop it.

I've insisted on washing the filthy clothes they came in and now I pick up a pair of their underwear, blue with green bears on them. Not only are they made for boys but they are made for penises, with a flap and everything.

Why do you need this flap hole? I ask. Is it, like, for fashion, or a dick?

They pause mid–cereal bite.

Sorry, I say.

I'm not, they say. Ask me anything you want. It's for both, they say.

A few hours later, Cara appears in the living room in the same pajama top but different earrings—big red lips made of clay. She and Beth wear the same cutoff jean shorts, so the same white fraying strings dangle down both of their thighs. She says good morning to me but not to Beth.

Ponies, she says. I want to see the ponies!

We load the dogs into my car and pull out of the development onto the two-lane road that takes us through the marsh and over the bridge to Chincoteague. Cara sits in the back with the dogs and babies them, feeling their fuzz and waving their paws.

Mike didn't want to come? she says.

Nah, I say. He's not much of a beach guy.

By now he'd be out in the garden, a thing he loves more than anything and only does when I am gone.

I pass Beth my jumbo Dunkin' iced coffee, and they settle it into my cupholder and tune the radio to my favorite heavy metal station. The fog has lifted early and it's sunny already. It's a good day.

Cara used to read a book about a pony who lived on Chincoteague, Beth says. She would read it every night before bed and even when her mom came to turn out the light she would keep reading it. She would stash a flashlight at the foot of her bed and read under the covers.

I already told her that, Cara says.

But Beth turns around from the passenger seat to smile at Cara anyway. They don't smile that much, so it's nice to see.

I wonder if I should feel bad, unfaithful in my affection for the Tomboy, who has no mother and once sent me a box of pears on Mother's Day. But in truth, I do not.

Let it go, I once said to Beth, of the Tomboy. Beth and the Tomboy had been standing by the garage for hours. Beth kept taking their baseball cap off, wiping their nose on their long-sleeve shirt, and putting their cap back on. The Tomboy stood there with her arms crossed over her small breasts. This was before they had opened up their relationship and the Tomboy had cheated on Beth—once, twice, who could say how many times? The Tomboy couldn't. Beth came back in by themself holding a small stick. They sat down at the table and began stripping the bark off the stick with a steak knife.

That's when I said it.

Yeah, Beth said, to this advice. Yeah. Their blue eyes were rimmed in red. I left them there when they turned the stick over and began stripping the other side. Later I heard them backing their car down the driveway. Three hours passed and then the phone rang, Beth calling from the dorms.

I can't let it go, Beth said. She loves me.

But do you love her? I asked.

I'm afraid, Beth said, but then stopped and started a new sentence. She loves me so much, Beth said.

I drive the Land Rover as far into the park as the road will let me and pull over onto the grassy shoulder, taking my place in a line of parked cars. Online, this spot was marked on the map as the best place to see ponies, so other people have the same idea.

We let the dogs run off-leash down the paved trail that winds in a lazy loop around the point. Small birds whistle overhead, hopping from tree to tree. Huge hawks appear low above us then slice upward into the sky. Cara wears brightly colored hiking boots but Beth is, as ever, in the black low-top Converse sneakers they have had since high school, and I worry that anything, anything at all, could break through that canvas and puncture them. A Delmarva fox squirrel, a strange gray creature that looks like a chinchilla with a fox's tail, shows off for us, eating acorns on a tree branch. I take Cara's arm by accident to stop her in her path when we come across a deer that has more horn than a doe but less than a stag. Perhaps it is a male deer whose antlers have fallen off and in their place are only these nubs. That's what Cara and I agree that it is.

Finally we reach the boardwalk and then the pony observation deck. Through the binoculars that Cara has brought precisely for this purpose, a gesture of preplanned hope that breaks my heart, we can see dots of white birds with pale pink beaks, more hawks. But no ponies.

Beth leans into the wooden railing and makes a good show of looking for them. Is that one? they say, putting their arm around Cara's shoulders.

Cara shrugs Beth's arm away and turns to face me.

Tell me, she says. What do you love about martial arts?

I pat my arm flesh—freckled, a little loose, but good, firm. I still don't know what this body is for. It's for kicking and punching, I guess, it's for swimming. How many times has Beth said, You're still young. Try it with someone else, anyone else besides Dad. I know some things that I like. I like the water in the shower to be really hot. I like it when the dogs walk over me when I'm sleeping, almost painful where their paws touch down with all that weight.

Oh, I dunno, I say. I like the structure and the routine. I like that it's a guarantee that I will be in my body for one hour each day.

Yeah, Cara says. I totally get that. I want that but haven't found my way in yet.

What about sex? Beth says a little loudly. You always say you feel in your body during sex.

Mmm, yes, Cara says, looking down at her feet and turning them out. But I wasn't gonna say that to your mom.

Mama is a citizen of this world, Beth says, smiling and putting their arm around me. We tell each other everything.

I pat their thigh.

Cara squints at us then and I wonder what she is thinking. And I think, *Good.* A little pushing back and forth between her and Beth might be good for all involved. Beth and the Tomboy are alike, even look alike, whereas Beth and Cara do not and are not.

No ponies, none at all. After an hour, Beth wants to stay and keep looking, has taken Cara's binoculars and is scanning the salt marsh, but Cara looks deflated and says it's alright, look at the dogs, they're thirsty, let's just go. We walk the rest of the loop and decide to break off down a small path to the point as a last-ditch effort.

If we can't give you ponies, we can at least give you ocean, Beth says.

We go from sun to shade then back to sun again. We walk through an open clearing that is charred black, burned on purpose, and then through a stand of pine trees. It smells like Christmas, and air freshener, all the things that are real and all the things that are fake.

The path spits us out onto a small muddy shore that smells salty. This, too, is not the ocean, only a hushed marshy inlet. Natty Boh cans, a piece of mattress foam, and a swath of metal mesh big as a cafeteria tray float and beach on the sand.

The wind blows harder and the sun gets hotter. Cara and Beth throw chunks of driftwood around for the dogs, who tire out quickly—they're prettier than they are sporty, Mike's idea to get huskies. Beth throws a big branch into the dirty water but the dogs won't chase, scared to put their bodies all the way in. Beth keeps pointing to the water and yelling at them, Go on, go on!

They're scared, Cara calls out. They don't want to.

So Beth takes their shoes off and goes after the branch themself, crashing through the salt cordgrass, grabbing it with a little *plunk*. Beth's shoulders and forearms are big now, and their white T-shirt and black hoodie are dry even as they come out of the water. I made them take martial arts as a kid to keep them from huffing aerosol. Then one day they said, Come with me.

Cara starts walking along the shoreline toward what looks like a wooden water tank in the distance and I find a log to sit on, figuring I'll give her and Beth a few minutes to walk together and maybe talk. But Beth sits down next to me instead.

I know you're dying to ask, Beth says. So go ahead.

My daughter, they know me.

Okay, I say. How does it work? Who do you love more? How do you find enough hours in the day? Where do you go to sleep? Where do you wake up?

They start on a long speech about how it doesn't have to be one thing or the other, how there can be enough love for all of us. But I interrupt them.

What did you mean about having to make something up to Cara?

I lied, they say. They told Cara they were going camping

with a friend when in fact they went camping with the Tomboy. Then they lied again. Then a few more times.

Why? I say. Isn't the idea total honesty, let the chips fall where they may?

Yes, Beth says. But I know it still hurts Cara. What she wants to practice and what she feels are sometimes not the same thing. Sometimes there is a gap there.

Ah, I say. And you?

I don't like hurting her, they say. Again they rub their eyes with the very tips of their fingers. When they stop, I see the skin of their finger pads has turned orange from all those sweet potatoes.

But maybe, Beth goes on, I think I don't hurt as much as other people. I simply tell myself, This does not hurt.

Does that work? I ask.

It works well enough, they say. But when they see I'm still looking, they smile at me. I'm okay, Mama, they say. Really.

And for a minute Beth is eight and I am twenty-eight and wondering whether to go and if so where, and we're sitting on the beach at Cape Henlopen. It was a hazy day, a failure. I asked Beth, Should I go, and if so, where? They looked up from the design they were drawing in the sand, and considered. They were squatting in boy swim shorts, no suit top. And why not? Their breasts were the same then as now—nothing.

Mama, they said. You're still young. You could go anyplace. Take Dad's car.

But where?

Philadelphia.

We had once watched together, while sucking pineapple popsicles, a documentary about that city, our neighbor to the north, a place of liberty and brothers and signed documents. Then Beth went there on a school trip without me. It was wonderful, they said when they returned. The edges of all their jeans were dipped in mud and they were so wiped from walking they passed out with their bedroom light on. I turned it off.

Cara is hollering and stumbling toward us. A pony! she says. A pony! Over there. Drinking.

Beth and I scramble to our feet and follow her around the shore, which bends, and when it straightens again Cara is right. There is one pony. Deep reddish color. Tail switching. Munching salt cord.

Good eye, I say.

Cara's plump cheeks flame with sun and energy. Beth rubs their hands up and down Cara's back and Cara pulls Beth's hands in to hold her around the waist.

Come closer, Cara says, calling out. Come closer, little pony. Come closer here to me.

The pony doesn't move.

Come on, I say to Cara. If we are very slow and quiet, we can touch it. You want to?

Cara nods. She squeezes both of Beth's orange hands, then brings them to her mouth and kisses them, as if every part of my child's body is precious and filled with luck. Then she lets Beth go and follows me.

We creep very quietly through the sand. Still the pony does not move. It flicks its tail at us, blinks its eyes. Holds its head very erect, listening.

That's right, I say. We won't hurt you.

Ohhh, Cara says, when she's almost close enough to touch the pony. Ohhh.

Then she is touching the pony, ever so lightly between its ears. She is running her hand along the pony's hard fur.

I look back at Beth. They have stayed where we were, feet in the wet sand, the canvas of their shoes surely soaked through by now. Their eyes are closed like they are praying or simply calm, free of anxiety. It is their calmness, their peace, how not afraid they are, that chills me and makes me shudder. My child is magic, cheating sorrow, bathing in love in a way the world has never known and will not allow.

Mama, Beth said that day at Cape Henlopen. You're beautiful.

But they didn't say it like a daughter—casual, like beauty was a thing we both had or wanted to have. They said it topless and squinting, sacred and serious as a son.

Also, they didn't say: Take me with you.

I WANT A FRIEND

Maybe it was only the mood I was in that night—bitter, biting, yet full of loose energy—that led me back to the queer bar, a place I'd sworn I'd never go again. By then I had no grand hopes left for love, but was propelled instead by quite another purpose: I wanted a friend. Not just any friend. I wanted *the* friend, the friend who is the stuff of movies and books and love songs—the friend who sees, the friend who gets, the friend to whom you have to explain nothing and who is yours until the end of time.

All afternoon and into the gloaming, I'd been lazing about the fourth-floor walk-up apartment where I was plant-sitting, watching TV on my laptop and polishing off a bottle of screw-top rosé, precisely the kind of blissful combination my other self disapproves of. What was the deal with Tony Soprano, finally and after all? So beautiful, so angry. Emails were piling up from the grant-writing job back in Philadelphia I was supposed to be doing but which the six-hour time difference made energetically impossible. By the time my coworkers were fully caffeinated and firing on all cylinders, I was lethargic and ready for cheese.

Then it was time to go. On the metro, two girls sat side by side in matching floral dresses and cursed each other over tiny hands made of butterfly wings. The exit tunnel and escalator smelled like important documents burning, which is the best description of Paris as a whole that I am capable of offering.

My potential new friend was a woman I'd met on Twitter when she'd liked a picture of my cat. Cute cat, she'd commented. What's his name?

I told her his name—yes, like the angel—and she'd barged into my DMs with a monologue about the Holy Trinity, which is my actual favorite subject to debate. Three into one, one into three. It makes no sense, yet it makes sense. *I agree, utterly and totally,* this woman said. She too was an American lingering in France rather than touristing, a lapsed academic. In her little photo, she wore a droopy yellow bow in her hair. Here, I remember thinking, was a person who did not play by the world's rules.

As usual, the filmmaker and her girlfriend stood in the street outside the bar smoking the cheapest possible cigarettes. They greeted me with kisses in a tired kind of way, turning their faces to mine so that only our chins touched. A few months ago, I had caused a lot of emotional trouble here for a friend of theirs, so I understood their hesitation.

The signs asking for donations to fund the bar's legal fees had come down, and I wondered what this meant. The bar had opened in a disreputable neighborhood that over time had become reputable, triggering a campaign from its new neighbors to close it down for reasons of sound and sexuality. But this argument does not play out the same way in France as it would in America, I have learned, for though the French surely have their own confusions of object and symbol, they are generally unimpressed by binary thinking. It's an immunity I am still trying to acquire.

Over my large plastic cup of good beer, I watched the butch-femme couples kiss each other with their tender fish mouths and surveyed the gaggles of androgynes in vests made from various shades of denim who occupied the couches in the graffiti-covered back room. I had the feeling again then, the only feeling that makes my other self shut up and listen.

When I was twenty-four, I was dating three people at once and then one of them, the one holding it all together, broke up with me, triggering a break not in my heart but in my mind. After a whole year of that feeling, I drove west from Philadelphia into the mountains until I arrived at my destination: a shooting range/gun store. GUNS, its big sign said, ALL SHAPES AND SIZES. I had called in advance about their requirements, and I knew I could be successful if I wanted to be. Success, in this context, would have been a lovely gun, a perfect right angle, very small and possibly silver, held to the right side of my head and then fired. Did I want to? My other self was silent when I pulled the car back onto the two-lane, back onto I-76, and silent through all the miles home. The decision was mine and mine alone.

. . .

According to the clock above the bathroom with pictures of birds for numbers, my potential new friend was late. I saw one girl I thought was cute, in a black button-up onesie—little tits, no bra—which was just the kind of garment I would like to wear but never would. By the time you got the pants on and fastened in just the right way, you'd have no energy left for the top.

Here is the thing: I had a friend once, for three years, mostly in Philadelphia, though she visited me in several of the temporary places I have lived, including here. One day it was all, Let's write our names on a cheap gold lock and lock it to this bridge. It was I who went to the general store in Belleville and bought the lock, but she who wrote the initials in Sharpie and plopped the little key into the water. To be fair, the lock was so cheap that the U of it kept coming out altogether, so I helped my friend jam it in once it was around the thin iron trestle. We also wrote vows, promising to bring more joy into each other's lives rather than less and to remind each other that we are both special and destined for great things. This is a kind of marriage, I said, and it means we are together now, until the end of time.

Okay, she said.

Maybe I should have clarified the terms, or picked up on my friend's hesitation. But there's a reason for that extra *F*—it's not "best friends for now, until we tire of each other." Object permanence, my other self was fond of telling me, is not your forte. She may have been right, that other self. Yet here is what she did not know: People leave. People quit. People pack up and move on.

My ex–best friend forever stayed with me at another temporary apartment, in Rome, for a week while deciding whether to leave her husband. My temporary cat, a brown floof with extra toes who belonged to an aged gay science fiction writer who had authored a cult classic, purred between her breasts.

It's been so long since I've felt free, she said. I've never told anyone that before.

I know, I said.

We ordered noodles delivered by an Italian man on a slick red scooter, and it was she, not I, who made the mocking comments about the likely size of his cock. We watched a movie about the Italian mafia, how it extends its tentacles into every corner of Italian life, even into the trash cans and the gardens.

Do you ever feel, she said, that your body is like a garden full of trash, and that the longer you live, the more trash you dig up, until you think you are done digging up trash and then you dig up the biggest piece of all?

Duh, I said.

All that night, as my ex–best friend and I lay turned away from each other in the science fiction writer's big bed, my other self spoke to me in aphorisms. *Keep no secrets, tell no lies; love is a verb, not a noun; if you love someone, set them free.* I didn't know how exactly these related to my situation, but I listened to her words, took what I wanted, and left the rest. I understood that there were some things—the institution of heterosexual marriage, for example—against which, if I fought, I would lose every time.

In the morning, my ex–best friend was no closer to a decision, so it was I who sent her packing back to America, land of so many husbands, with half a loaf of the banana bread we'd made. *Meow,* the cat said when she left with her big shiny backpack, which protected all her most important belongings from the elements—her grid-lined notebooks and her Muji pens and her big jade necklace and her tarot cards and her rock that I had given her, which absorbed her sadness. *Meow,* the cat said again when she called to say she had decided to stay with her husband and marry him again in her mind. There was static in the connection, my other self trying to speak. I spoke over it.

But what about how he tramples your spirit? I said.

I never said that, she said.

Hadn't she?

First came the series of small miscommunications, then the one very bad lunch at the bakery on the avenue in West Philadelphia, then finally the email: Never call me again. Don't text. Don't tweet. Don't like me, don't tell my story.

I know I am no picnic to love—that much has been made abundantly clear time and again—but this, I thought, I would never, as long as I lived, understand. I was right, as I still do not understand it. What kind of person slams the door on love in so loud a manner, plus so quick, and forever? What kind of person puts all their troubled blood into a single arm and then cuts off the arm? Whack.

There was no continuity, there was no longevity, there was no forgiveness, it seemed. The snake did not eat its tail but instead kept eating pieces of experience and shitting them out. I felt like that snake—renewed and empty, with no direction to go but forward. How many times had I moved, how many cities had I plowed through in the decade between childhood and real life? Paris was the fifth or the sixth, depending on your definition of residency.

While I sat waiting in the queer bar, I drank from my big plastic cup of beer and listened to the music play. The clock had left its position at the blue jay and now pointed to a brown speckled fowl with luxurious plumage. I opened the glass door and stood in the street. The bouncer had taken off her suspenders and they fell onto her big thighs. I asked the filmmaker if she had a cigarette. She gave me one and even offered to light it for me.

Where have you been? she asked in English, without too much meanness. We've worried.

Oh, here and there, I said. The university near my apartment has been on strike so I've been listening to all the speeches.

Don't listen too hard, she said. Eventually, it's just the same guy, over and over again. She smiled. *Viens avec nous,* she said, gesturing to her girlfriend and then down the street. We're going for falafel. She crushed her cigarette beneath her Converse shoe.

My ex–best friend forever had called these Chuck Taylors because she is from the Midwest, though there could have been some other reason.

I can't, I said. I'm waiting for someone.

I watched them turn the corner and then I watched two baby dykes make out furiously against the dirty window of the laundry next door. The streets were dark and friendly and the world was truly huge and glittering, I remembered, despite the way it had been treating me.

She never showed, that new friend. Later, a message appeared saying that she had been caught in a terrible rainstorm (she was taking the metro in from *la banlieue*) and asked if we could reschedule—"a raincheck!" Haha, my other self said, what a dumb joke.

No, I wrote back.

I never did find another friend like the one I'd lost, and if I had known that then like I know it now, I would not have gone on living. But it is possible, I have discovered, to supply that kind of friendship to oneself, if you work very hard at it and practice every day. I'm doing it now, even as we have been talking all this time, even with you here.

LANTERNFLY

A week into my sojourn with Rob, we'd established a routine: black coffee in his swan mug; the slow, puffing, two-block walk to the beach; the selection of the day's spot and the digging of the hole for the umbrella; the rise and fall of a book on each of our bellies; lunch from the cooler and then a nap when the sky turned hazy. By late afternoon, Rob would wobble to the beach snack bar, returning with a sheaf of fries for him and a Chipwich for me. Though covered in a fine layer of ice crystals, the Chipwich was soon soft. I ate the edges first, the mini chocolate chips crunching between my back molars.

Good? Rob asked as I scraped bits of wet cookie from my fingertips with my teeth.

His gray beard covered the broad space between his nipples and fluttered in the ocean wind. Otherwise, he resembled a Black Mr. Potato Head—all belly, hat, sunglasses, and cheetah-print sneakers, which he wore everywhere, even here in the sand.

Good, I said.

Rob was Robert Bunch, the famous science-fiction writer,

and I was supposed to be assisting him with his research, though this was as far as the assisting had gone.

I'd met Rob at an event hosted by the City University's graduate program for creative writing, where he taught and where my friend Cara had just finished her MFA—a big deal for her, her second crack at one (her first had been in studio art; a long yarn, she'd said several times, though she'd never unwound it). I'd read all of Rob's books at the library where I worked and was a fan. What if there was a world without gender and suffering? That sort of thing. After the readings, Cara's entourage stood at a folding table covered in a bright red cloth where a cake—purple icing with white flourishes—was being carved up.

What's the cake for? I asked.

Me, Rob said. He was suddenly beside me wearing a shirt patterned with human tongues. I'm retiring, he said. Then, quieter: Not of my own accord.

I offered my congratulations, but he waved them off. You're the only one here who looks like fun, Rob said.

Thank you, I said. What happened to fun?

The answer to this question is elusive to me, he said. I often bring my own.

From a neon-green tote bag splashed with glitter, he produced two feathered face masks and held one out to me. Apparently, he and his deceased wife, a once-famous poet and critic, had worn them to a costume party in the 1970s. Today was their anniversary, he told me, and he was feeling nostalgic. I accepted the mask, placing it over my head, careful not to break the string, which was losing its elasticity. His whole deal charmed me. At the end of the night, as we stood face-to-face in masks of love, he asked me to spend the month of August with him at the Jersey Shore.

Jules, no! Cara exclaimed once we were on the train going south so that we could eventually switch to a trolley that would go west.

I like him, I replied. Plus he'd pay me handsomely.

He's not a good person, Cara said. He barely taught us. Fell asleep in class. He claimed it was jet lag from all the travel, but for two years? Word is he sleeps with all his assistants, and one time I saw him at the Daily Grind with no less than six twinks.

Not opposed, I said, though I see myself as more of an otter.

Already I was starting to speak like Rob, as if I was being interviewed on a radio show or expecting to be recorded for posterity. His voice reminded me of someone and it wasn't until I was standing in my dark apartment and running the tap that I realized who it was: the voice that had recently started to speak from inside my own skull. If I ran down the stairs in my apartment building too jauntily, the voice said, *And where, pray tell, do you think you're going?* When I thought about signing up for a painting class at the art center in my neighborhood, the voice said, *I own you, and all you might make out of what you've been given.*

What had I been given? I had been given good hands, small fingers, and long nail beds that were always remarked on when I got a manicure. A good public education at a central New Jersey high school and a good public education at an affordable state university where there had been a cow you could see inside of—part of its side had been cut away and replaced with clear plexiglass—who ambled around the agricultural school campus. There was the small intestine, and there was the blood and the bile. I'd drawn that cow in my drawing class and been praised for it, a little but not too much, which was good for me. I'd been given this body, not the wrong one exactly, but not the right one either. I had arrived in my late twenties with a good job as a city branch librarian and good friends and a good apartment, the first-floor rear of a big Victorian where I made extra money working as the property manager. My overhead was low, I regularly sucked the dicks of Penn lacrosse bros when I wanted to, and there was a farmers' market nearby for flowers and vegetables which I bought from a hot guy who drove a motorcycle and towed his wares behind him in a little wagon. But then I'd gotten top surgery and the voice had begun.

I own the bulldozer, it said as I stood in my kitchen in the dark, drinking a glass of water. *I own the chains.*

The family in front of Rob and me packed up their beach gear and was promptly replaced by a late-in-the-day group of friends—four straight white couples who separated quickly into gendered semicircles, the women all in black bikinis of different strap thicknesses and ass exposure, the men taking turns slapping a Bluetooth speaker shaped like a basketball.

From underneath his faded green bucket hat, Rob opened first one eye then the other. The skin of his pectorals draped like fabric; his nipples kissed the crest of his round stomach.

Alas, he said, inspecting our new neighbors. A terrible turn of events. To the water go I. Care to join me?

This was not really a question, as his comfort and safety were essential elements of my employment. Rob walked very slowly, his legs perhaps no longer able to bend at the knee. He was eighty-four years old and prone to falling—timber style—especially when rising from sitting to standing. As we maneuvered down the bank of sand, I offered my arm and his long fingers curled around my bicep. I could feel the sharp and brittle nails digging into my skin.

Strong boy, he said.

I was a boy, but I sometimes forgot to expect the word. This was only my second summer going shirtless; an image rose up from the previous year, also on the Jersey Shore but under much more humble circumstances—a day trip with Cara and her housemates, Cara feeding me grapes and beef jerky and making a fuss over applying a mineral-based sunscreen to my scars.

Rob and I stood at the water's edge. His swim trunks were yellow and shiny like a fisherman's coat. Two brown teens held hands and ran into the water together, jumping a small wave in unison. A young white guy with a hard glistening chest and a neck tattoo kicked the water as if testing its hostility against his own.

Rob suddenly lifted his foot and made a small noise. At first I thought he'd been bitten or stung, but then he pointed at something down in the wet sand: bulbous body, creeping slowly on long front legs and short back ones, a flash of red.

A spotted lanternfly—an invasive insect we were all supposed to be killing on sight. I dropped Rob's arm and snatched up the bug, ready to squish it between my palms.

No! Rob cried. Do not!

He lifted a delicate index finger.

Look, he said, pointing. Look at that color. Incredible.

In my hands, the insect's little legs thrashed, tickling me.

Give it here, Rob said.

I swam parallel to the shore, raising my head every now and then to check that Rob was still there on the sand, speaking to his fly, but he always was. I did little flips and dips in the water, like an otter. If a man on vacation with his wife and son should happen to look my way, so be it, but I wasn't chasing looks.

I'd heard that, aside from the emotional, the ocean's restorative properties are mainly mineral—the white popping and fizzing of the surf is minerals breaking apart in the spray. I used my hands to bring cupfuls of water to my face and breathed in. After so many months of working in the library and recovering from surgery, I could use all the minerals I could get.

I couldn't see my feet through the murky water, but they were there, their little knuckles all going in different directions. Sometimes I felt that if I could get these strange feet straightened out, I could find my life: a man and a thing to do, or possibly a man who would give me a thing to do. I'd tried to have sex with the owner of my building, but I'd misread the cues. One moment he was asking me to mow the lawn and I was doing it, and the next he was sitting on my couch with his legs spread apart. I went and kneeled on the floor between his legs and he just looked at me. I put my hand on the breast pocket of his shirt like a golden retriever giving paw. We sat there for a long time before he told me to stand up in a low sexy voice that I'd thought meant yes and then he crossed the room and left and I realized it meant no.

When I looked back at the beach, Rob was waving me out.

That night, Rob skipped our nightly cocktail on the porch and even took the salmon and asparagus I'd prepared to his office instead of to the living room, where we'd been watching a new television show about a beautiful male chef who has been wounded by his dead brother and by the world. Chefing was the opposite of being wounded, this show seemed to argue. To chef properly, it was important to wake up at a regular time, to appear clean and follow the rules, and to speak to people with respect, no matter how lowly the food function they performed. As I watched the show, I felt inspired. I too could go to sleep at a reasonable hour. I could stack forks devoid of spots. I could listen to bad pop music and, via its energy, be reborn.

I was halfway through an episode alone when I heard the hunt-and-peck of Rob on his sticky keyboard. I'd taken the plastic cover off his ancient square desktop computer when we'd arrived, but he'd assured me he probably wouldn't use it. Now he was using it—damn was he using it. I finished the show, smoked a pre-roll on the porch, refilled my water bottle, and took it to bed with me. The sun had drained me like a raisin, but with fluid and rest I would become a grape again. When I passed the closed door of Rob's office, the light was still on.

It will be a new trilogy, he said the next morning over breakfast. The first one will be called *Lanternfly.*

Not *Spotted Lanternfly*?

Just *Lanternfly.* The bugs hitch rides from China or Vietnam or are blown inland by winds and appear in brand new countries such as the United States. They like a tree called Tree of Heaven, which is perhaps what I'll call the second one.

How exciting, I said.

How wretched, he said.

Meaning?

Well, now my vacation is ruined. I've got to work. You'll have to beach without me.

Oh, I said. Won't you want lunch?

He waved his hand. When I am in the throes, I hardly eat, he said. Coffee and dinner will be sufficient. Protein-heavy, please. Eggs. Canned fish. Seltzer water. Crackers.

I got a pen and made a list on the back of an envelope.

But there is one other thing. He opened his mouth, then closed it again.

Sex, he said finally. I'll need to have some. A lot, actually. Sometimes several times a day.

I looked at the linen shirt he was wearing, white with orange stripes, and imagined removing it from his back. Unbuttoning the buttons, folding it neatly. He would see my feet. Perhaps he would touch them.

Not with you, obviously, he said. There's an application, as I understand it. On the phone. But I'll need your help.

I poured us second cups of coffee and we relocated to the back garden, where I could vape and he could run his fingers over the thick green skin of the basil plants. The day had started out cloudy but was in a transitional phase now, warm and about to become right. If we had been on the beach, we would have burned.

I knew his age, so I input that first.

Position, I read aloud. Top. Vers Top. Versatile. Vers Bottom. Bottom. Side.

As in?

I chose my words carefully.

Any more options?

Yes, one. Not Specified.

That, he said.

We discussed the pros and cons of face pictures, dick pictures, and the strikes against him in this context: old, fat, Black.

Half Black, he said.

Want me to write that?

No, he said. Put my face. And my books. Put the titles. Write that my fingers are nimble and my soul is wide. Say I will tell them stories.

I checked some boxes and unchecked others. I felt hopeful for him, and also ashamed. This was a private activity, an activity I'd never shared with anyone. I was used to thinking of sex as a kind of errand, something I did in advance so I wouldn't be hungry later. But here was Rob, starving.

Here, I said, handing the phone to him.

Now what? he said.

Now we wait, I said, and we look.

He gave the phone back to me. You'll look for me, he said. I'll tell you what I like. I like all men, it doesn't matter what size or shape. Tall men have a certain something, like trees. Short men will work harder, like me. I work very, very hard. Fat men have a better touch, a natural instinct for the sensations of flesh. Thin men are more aerodynamic and can see every part of their bodies. They are familiar, perhaps too familiar with everything, but this self-knowledge can be interesting. The only thing is I'll want time. None of this wham-bam-thank-you-ma'am. I can't do it just like that. I'll want to give them wine, I'll want to give them a cookie, I'll want to listen to records.

I think I understand, I said. There's a word for that now, it's—

But Rob just waved his hand again. No, he said, there's no word.

. . .

I lay on the beach, having swum a long time and exuberantly, now that I didn't have to watch Rob. My legs felt gelatinous and my eyelashes dripped water. There was extra breath in my body.

I had used the app so many times, but swiping on Rob's account on Rob's behalf made it new again. I was reminded of my very first days in the app, when I would pull a move each time. I would leave something at his place—a sock, or a book, or a stud earring. *Hey you,* I'd text. *Did I leave my earring?* So cute. I was cute for a long time before I became what I am now. *No,* they'd always text back, though I knew I had. I imagined these men wearing my earrings, reading my books, smelling my socks.

Brian was the first man I messaged as Rob who messaged me back. He had slightly crowded bottom teeth, bleached blond hair, and lived nearby in Point Pleasant. *My place only,* I wrote in Rob's voice, *as traveling is no longer easy for me.*

Tonight? he replied, with a semicolon-parenthesis winky face. His profile said he was thirty-two, but I knew from this emoticon that he was at least in his forties.

Tonight, I agreed.

When I got back to the house, I knocked on Rob's door. He was typing away, his eggs from the morning still untouched.

If you were a caterpillar, he asked me, what would your name be?

Fred, I said.

Rob thought about it for a moment, his fingers paused on the keys. Alright, he said. Fred.

You've got a guest tonight, I said. Or at least I think you do.

Wonderful, Rob said. When he arrives, send him right in.

Brian was half an hour late. Through the bottom half of the screen door, I watched the nose of his Dodge Charger appear by the curb. People were coming back from the beach and dogs were getting their evening jaunts as Brian's long tanned legs and feet, somewhat pigeon-toed and bare in cheap plastic flip-flops, came up our stairs.

Well, Brian said, looking me up and down. This is a bit of a bait and switch.

From the living room with its many woven rugs and chenille pillows and dark wood paneling stained almost black so that the whorls and eddies made concentric ovals like the rings of Saturn, I listened to the sounds emanating from Rob's bedroom. A heavy item of furniture with trinkets atop it wobbled, then shook. The bed squeaked against its springs, then screeched across the floor. Something heavy—a stack of books, possibly—hit the floor and dispersed into its individual parts. I imagined pushing, I imagined shoving and biting. I imagined *bend over* and *hold your ankles* and *relax* and *let me do it*. I imagined a dynamic full of flirting and teasing despite the sounds that suggested a more straightforward order of things. I could have put my noise-canceling headphones on at any point. I had them, right there on the table. On the TV, the chef finally runs into his childhood sweetheart in the frozen aisle of the grocery store. She's gorgeous, funny, gets him. She opens the frozen case door so now a pane of glass is separating them. He can't speak.

Brian came downstairs around midnight. The windows were open and air was coming in, air straight from the ocean. Brian looked the same, if slightly greasier. He had removed the light shirt he'd been wearing when he came in and now wore only a tank top, so I could see his arms, which were lightly muscled. He stood in the dark foyer, where Rob insisted the beach passes be kept in a tiny wooden box. The chairs and umbrella were leaning there too.

Damn, Brian said, and ran a hand through his hair. He glanced upstairs and looked like he was going to say something else.

The voice filled in the silence. *You,* the voice said to me, *will never be one of the holy nor the beautiful.*

Damn, Brian said again, then pushed through the screen door.

I was back on the app before Brian's flip-flops hit the pavement.

Since Brian had been so tall and wholesome, now I wanted someone short and swarthy and with more personality. I wanted someone I could share a joint with, someone who would sit with me afterward and offer specific, sensual details.

As Rob listened to *Dreamgirls: Original Broadway Cast Album,* I found and began messaging with Eli. It was his choice of *Not Specified* and predilection for gentlemen over sixty-five that drew him into my net. But I'd be lying if I said that I didn't take a certain interest in the fact that he, too, was trans. His name made it obvious, also his scars—in one picture of him smiling on the beach, I could see he had the kind of straight-across incisions they were doing in the 2010s, with folds of flesh near the armpits that people called "dog ears," a thing I had been told used to happen a lot, especially for bigger guys like him. I bet he'd even had to stay overnight in the hospital, a prospect I'd told Cara would nix the whole procedure for me.

Hello, I wrote. *Is 84 too far over 65?*

Yum, he responded.

The next morning, Rob was up before I was, preparing the coffee himself. He was more than a little bit blind and, as he hummed to himself, I repositioned the grounds in the press and recaptured all that had escaped.

Good? I asked him.

Very good, he said. My blood feels thin. As in, flowing.

Rob worked and I beached, showered, and prepared an early dinner, which Rob took upstairs and I ate on the wicker porch couch. The church that played Methodist hymns in bell form was chiming seven o'clock when a silver car slowed in front of the house, even though we'd said half past.

Hey, thanks, Eli yelled as he came around the car's nose.

The driver raised her hand, then accelerated down the wide street toward the ocean.

Eli was older than me, probably late thirties, short, thick, with a shaved head.

You must be Jules, Eli said. I nodded.

Get a hit? he asked, and I offered the joint.

Eli took it, still standing. His arms in his yellow T-shirt were fatter than mine and limper. So, you and him, like?

No, I said. I just help out.

That's nice, Eli said. He took another hit, kept it in his mouth, and passed the joint back to me. I do that for my grandpa, he said. Not in, like, the same way. My grandpa needs to get the baseball score but can't find the buttons.

Sure, I said.

Eli paused. You trans?

Yeah, I said.

Cool, Eli said.

Well, I said. Rob's upstairs.

This time, I heard nothing for a long time, and then I heard something, very suddenly. What I heard was Eli crying out and out and out and out. He was yelling Jesus. For some reason, I wondered if Eli, too, had been raised Catholic. A lot of trans guys I know were raised Catholic, a tradition that seemed to prepare you well to transform and then transform again, but which never, it seemed, left you.

Don't you dare wonder, my voice said. *Don't inquire. Don't long to know.*

As I listened and watched my show—now the chef was choosing plates and silverware and glassware for his future restaurant, one that would bear his name and his name only—I had the screen door open. The weather turned, growing cooler, then cooler still. At first I thought, when it starts to rain I will close the door. But then it began to rain and I did not close the door. Upstairs, Eli was still calling out. But instead of Jesus now he was saying God. Oh God, he was saying. My God. It began to rain harder and the trees began to blow around outside, a big beach-town storm rolling in. I could see the shine of water coming through the screen door, then a small pool of water accumulating on the hardwood floor. A chill ran through me. My feet, with all the trouble they caused me, were cold. Still I did not get up to close the door.

I lay there all night, and all night Eli did not come down the stairs. I wondered what they were doing for so many hours, though I knew. Sleeping and waking, touching and holding. In my mind, I made a list. I thought: If I can lie here all night without moving from my post, God grant me these ten wishes. 1) To never hear the voice again, or the voice of any god. 2) To find something else to believe in, for example the books in my library, but better. 3) To be able to go swimming at the beach without being ashamed of my feet, or just generally to find myself beautiful. 4) For Rob to touch me just once, to send some of his intergalactic knowledge my way. 5) To make one good work of art in my life, a drawing maybe, or a painting, one that has the effect of making people want to sing along, like an Alanis Morissette song from *Jagged Little Pill,* which was released the year I was born and which my mother loved and played to me in utero. 6) To love my friends better—Cara, for example, to really truly love her instead of loving her halfway. Love curdles when it is not expressed, goes rancid, and there are many years of such expired love that I still have stored up somewhere. 7) To be able to sleep without the assistance of drugs. 8) To one day own a beach house like this beach house, so I can access the minerals of the ocean even as I too approach death. 9) For it to be sunny tomorrow. 10) I could think of nothing else. I was out of wishes.

In the morning it was still raining and I woke to Eli and Rob's voices in the next room. They were talking quietly and laughing, like they were already boyfriends.

When I walked in, Eli was telling the kitchen that he was an acupuncturist in Asbury Park and had opened his own shop.

Hung out a shingle, Eli said, if you will.

I will, Rob said, wiggling his bushy white eyebrows.

I could give you a treatment if you want, Eli said to me.

For what?

For whatever you need. I promised Rob one for his back.

While I cleaned up the breakfast dishes, I watched Rob remove his shirt and lie facedown on the couch where I had been all night. I had touched those white linen cushions and that thin cotton bedspread he was now touching with the aging skin of his stomach and chest and hands. They were his cushions and bedspread after all; my skin and wishes had only been visiting.

This is war medicine, Eli said. Meant to help you feel better quick. It's not sit-in-your-chair-at-a-spa-and-feel-nice medicine.

Very good, Rob said. Begin.

Instead of inserting many needles and leaving them there, as I was expecting, Eli took one needle and jammed it into Rob's back many times. Rob winced in pain—ah, eh, oh, ooh—and Eli gave commentary validating this pain—Ooh yeah that one's gotta hurt and Damn that was so sticky, did you feel how sticky that one was?

Afterward, Rob lay very still, even long after Eli said, OK! Feel free to get up now! Eli turned to look at me in the kitchen, where I was still putting away the pots and pans. I stopped and looked back. I made a face like, Who knows? But I went over to Rob and crouched down next to him.

I'm alright, Rob said. Very excellent, actually. Now leave me, please.

What about you? Eli whispered to me in the kitchen. I can give you a treatment upstairs.

I'm good, I said.

Come on, Eli said. At the very least it will give you a great nap. Like—dead out.

Upstairs, I sat at the head of my bed and Eli sat at the foot, arranging his little supplies.

So tell me all your problems, Eli said with a laugh.

Physical or mental?

Aha, Eli said. There's your first mistake. Chinese medicine doesn't see them as separate.

Right, I said. Well, I've been having trouble sleeping.

Cool, Eli said. I can definitely give you a treatment for that.

I took my shirt off and lay down on my back. Eli walked

slowly along the edge of the bed and opened larger and then smaller ziplock bags. Leaning over me, he placed one needle between my eyebrows.

Wow, he said. Your scars look great. You healed, like, perfectly. You're lucky.

Thanks, I said. I'm still getting used to everything.

Oh I know, Eli said. It took me years. I was twenty-seven when I had my surgery, so about ten years ago. He put a needle behind one of my ears.

I was twenty-seven too, I said. Last year.

Nice, Eli said. Twenty-seven club. He put a needle behind my other ear.

Isn't it so weird? Eli said. Like we had tits and now we don't. That took me forever to work through.

How do you mean? I asked.

Eli took his time answering, inserting needles near the bony part of my wrists.

Hmm, Eli said, straightening up. I guess I just mean the physical reality of it. I read a ton and watched a ton of videos and it's, like, insane. It's so cool. The chest is full of all these globby white sacks of fat. They cut out a whole glop of breast tissue and then they sew you back up. You feel like a Frankenstein. Then you feel fantastic.

I was too scared to watch any videos, I said.

Oh no, you gotta, he said. It's incredible what they do, the technology, and it's only gotten better, obviously. But it was weird, like, not knowing where I was while they were doing the surgery. I don't remember it, but my body was there. And then when I woke up, you want to know what happened?

OK, I said, though I didn't.

Eli slid a needle into my right ankle. He said, I kept asking the nurses where my chest flesh went. He laughed and pierced my left ankle. I felt nothing.

I kept asking them, But where does it go? What did you do with it? They kept patting me on the shoulder and saying that it was okay and that the surgery had gone well. Apparently I was really insistent. Next thing I remember I was back home with my boyfriend at the time and there was a note from my doctor. It said, *Please convey to Eli that removed breast tissue is typically sent to a lab for cancer testing and then incinerated.*

Incinerated? I said as Eli put a needle into the crevice between my fucked-up right big toe and second toe.

Yeah, Eli said. They burn it. Isn't that crazy? Eli stuck a needle between the toes of my other foot.

Crazy, I said.

Eli set a timer on my phone and lowered the shades. He stood in the doorway of my room.

Bye, Jules, Eli said. Drink a lot of water.

I came downstairs a while later, and Rob was still lying on the couch, eyes closed.

When he finally opened them, he wanted to talk. He wanted to tell me about *Lanternfly* and ask for my help. Finally, I thought, we would begin.

What if, he said, what if it was set in a world where, right before you die, all the people you thought you'd lost were returned to you?

As in?

As in, the dead and the living, the living but distant from you. The people you bullied in school or who bullied you. The friends you fell out with because you didn't like their partners or because you had a kid and they didn't or they published a book and you didn't. The childhood best friend who moved away to Omaha because her dad got a job there. The boy you had a crush on in high school who overdosed on heroin in the bathtub. The gentle boy from your college English class who grew up to be a hard-nosed investment banker. The fellow from grad school who wouldn't use a condom with your friend.

And? I said again. So they come back, and then what?

So each one is a lanternfly. Each one appears to my protagonist before he dies and must be dealt with.

Dealt with how?

Remembered, he said. Spoken to. What I'm seeing is a scene of my protagonist on a city street with a whole swarm of spotted lanternflies. A swarm of memories.

I like it, I said.

Also, I said, why do you need sex to write?

The tightness, he said. And the looseness. It knocks something free. Some calmer and stranger energy that is also less strange. After orgasm the mind is clear. After orgasm, who wants to talk on the telephone?

True enough, I said. But why not just masturbate? Why do you need there to be men?

He smiled. I like to speak and be spoken to, pushed around

a little bit. What is sex if not being contacted by a foreign body, perhaps from outer space? It makes one feel a little less alone, no?

Yes, I said, thinking of my voice.

I went to the grocery store and bought all the luxurious stone fruits and all the specialty cheeses with Rob's credit card. Popcorn coated in pink Himalayan sea salt. Flowers. If Rob would not indulge, I would for the both of us.

Call Eli, Rob said as I was unloading everything.

Within an hour, Eli was back, bearing crabs. The crab clusters were from Alaska, not from New Jersey, but their pink flesh and knobby shells created a feeling of freshness and regional specificity. I looked for newspaper around the house but found none so Rob sent me upstairs to raid his office.

Take the drafts, he said. Leave the notes.

The room was covered in a fine film of dust. On the desk sat the outdated computer, a box labeled NOTES, and a series of small treasures, or talismans. A round black stone, so shiny it looked lacquered. A bird's nest with a paper-thin egg in it. A miniature wooden house covered in cheap pink gemstones. The house had a little porch with steps and everything. On the steps were little figurines—one that looked like Rob, and three others: a white woman and two little boys.

Eli showed us how to dismember and eat the crab by gently breaking the shell with your fingers and then feeling for the meat.

You've got to tug oh so lightly to get the whole leg out in one piece, he said. Like so.

Rob's fingers had lost much of their dexterity, so after a few tries I stepped in.

Good boy, Rob said to me as I pulled a tender pink chunk from the biggest leg. Well done, he said as I dunked it in butter and handed it to him.

With every drop of butter that landed on the paper, more of Rob's novel became visible, each word revealed in reverse.

After dinner, Rob opened all the windows and put a record on the ancient turntable. Rob and Eli were on the couch, Eli sitting upright drinking a cocktail and Rob lying down with his head in Eli's lap. He wasn't wearing any socks and I watched him move his toes to the beat.

I wish we had a dog, Eli said. A dog would complete this feeling.

What feeling is that? Rob asked.

Boys having fun, Eli said. Boys having entirely too much fun. We could make a dog dance or roll over.

We had a dog for many years, Rob said. Terry and I and the boys. He was a scruffy little terrier by the name of Pluto. But he couldn't do any tricks or anything. He never listened to us when we called, never took to his name.

I wish he were here now, Eli said. Pluto! Pluto!

And then Rob was sitting up.

The lanternfly was walking carefully along the window ledge.

I've got it! Eli said, taking up a hardback book.

No! Rob and I called out together.

Rob swooped for the insect and cupped it between his palms. He sat down on the couch, holding it, and began to cry. First he cried slow tears. Eli sat beside him and rubbed his back while I hovered uselessly. Then Rob straight-up wept, big boo-hoos.

Oh, honey, Eli said. What is it?

I miss my sons, Rob sobbed. My boys!

We could call them, Eli suggested. Here, let me see your phone.

No, no, Rob said, still weeping. I don't want to bother them. I miss when they were young and snuggled me. I miss my wife. I miss my Terry.

Eli and I looked at each other. Eli rubbed Rob's back again. I'm old! Rob said. My body is breaking down.

You're still plenty limber, Eli said, kissing him on the cheek.

They even took my job from me! Rob blubbered. The only job I've ever known.

Eli went to get Rob a tissue.

Those people at the university, I said. They're idiots.

Rob looked up at me then, and smiled a little. True, he said.

After nose blowing and a glass of water, Rob stopped crying. He lifted his T-shirt to dry his eyes, exposing his soft belly.

What do you think it means? Eli asked, after some time. You're writing a book about lanternflies, and lo, a lanternfly appears!

He was asking with seriousness, with a serious face and a serious heart, and I saw then that this was the reason Rob was having sex with him and not me. I would never be able to ask such a stupid question.

After we all smoked a good bit, Rob wanted to eat ice cream. I offered to bring the car around, but Rob said no, it was a nice night and he wanted to walk. The town had once been a Methodist camp and tonight was Illumination Night, so everyone was out and about, paper lanterns lighting up the exteriors of their little pink and green and yellow gingerbread houses. But the line for the ice-cream parlor wrapped around the corner, past the historical society and the mermaid store, and Rob was soon hunching over and holding his back.

You guys sit, Eli offered valiantly. Give me your orders.

Kids wore glow-in-the-dark bracelets and necklaces and some were even breaking them and smearing the luminescent chemicals on their lips and arms. At the edge of the park, I stood over Rob's seated form on a bench.

I was thinking, Rob said, keeping his eyes level and straight ahead, that the narrator of *Lanternfly* will be not quite dead, but almost there, in the place the Buddhists call the Bardo.

That could work, I said. I'd read that.

It's been done before, he said. As everything worth doing has. But this narrator hasn't lived a usual life. He's had relations with people of both genders. He's lived first as one sex, and then as another. He has had more life than most are ever allowed, so it takes him a long time to leave the Bardo. He's wrestling in there, thinking and greeting all the people, er, insects, from every phase of his life to another and he's fighting, really and truly fighting, to stay alive. It will take three books for him to die, but he is going to die, eventually.

He's stuck, I said. That's interesting. I crouched down so I could be lower than Rob, as I deserved.

Sit, Rob said. Come sit on this bench with me.

I sat.

I see that you are suffering, Rob said.

I swallowed.

I can't pretend to know the cause and I can't solve it. You're young, not even thirty, and maybe you think the big things have come and gone already, but they haven't. They're about to come, they're coming, the big changes. The thirties, the forties. Even the fifties.

What about punishment? I said. Don't you think we will be punished if we change too many times?

How many times is too many? Punished by whom? Oh my, you really are a Catholic.

And after the fifties?

The sixties, the seventies. Maybe they're more like the twenties, Rob said. A certain hunger comes back, an urgency. I'm a horny young boy again.

I think, maybe, I'd like to live a long time, I said. That's a new development.

Rob tugged on his beard approvingly.

I'm calling the character in my trilogy Jules, he said. And

giving him your—how do we say?—unusual feet. Also your beautiful hands.

Wow, I said. I don't know what to say.

And I'm putting in that strange story about the cow with the hole in its side, was it?

Window, I said. Clear.

Right, he said. Disgusting. I would have stood there for hours, watching the intestines.

I did, I said.

Fluffy, tall dogs darted in and out of the bushes, and in the gazebo a band of three blond teenaged girls set up electric guitars and began to play a hymn. I caught the words *Messiah* and *prince of peace.*

Rob closed his eyes. He covered my hand with his, clumsily, his hand half on my hand and half on the wooden surface of the bench. His skin was warm and dry.

Eli came striding across the grass then, three double-scoop ice-cream cones smushed together in a great tower. I had ordered espresso chip and black raspberry, and whether from the anticipation or the THC or both, my mouth flooded with sour moisture. The teens sang louder and louder in one high, thin voice that I did not believe in, but this nonbelief did not prevent my noticing that the tune was sweet and pleasing to my ears.

I'm a bit scared, Rob said. Of the next phase of matter. Not too much, he said. But a little.

Me too, I said.

The weed had left a rancid taste in my mouth, but it would

soon be washed away by cream. Rob lifted his hand away from mine as Eli approached. I didn't move. I knew that Rob could redeem me in his books, or hurt me, but whatever form I took next in life, he would not be able to imagine it. That work was all mine.

SWIFFER GIRL

Do you remember Swiffer Girl? I remember that she existed years ago, back before I felt every man I passed in the sunshine like a mortal enemy, back before college, before moving to six cities in six years, before the friend I lost, before good sex and good love, before *misogyny* and *relationship anarchy* and *intersectionality* and all the other language I've learned to use to describe experience. I never really "got sober" the way other people did, just met a woman named Bree who has a rare condition that makes her allergic to alcohol and bought a house with her. There was no dramatic quitting, no taking out a trash bag heavy with clear glass bottles, no standing up at meetings to repeat the same confession, just a gradual secretion via perspiration and rehydration. Slowly, the booze left my bloodstream and was replaced by other liquids—seltzer, chocolate milk, Lemon Zinger tea. I forgot Swiffer Girl for years. Then I didn't.

Bree says that being in water is the only thing that makes having a body not hell. Fair enough, though I don't swim—city kid, never learned.

It's warm, the first warm Saturday of the year, so as a little treat we're at a new pool that just opened on the roof of a fancy apartment building up Broad Street from our house. I watch Bree swim laps, tracking the red strings at the back of her neck as they float over the surface of the water. Bree comes to the pool's edge close to where I am reclining, stacks her forearms, rests her head on top, and closes her eyes.

This, she says, is the nicest pool I've ever swum in.

Ever?

She nods solemnly.

Elaborate.

The water feels thick but not gooey. Salt, no chlorine. Heated but not too hot.

I'm happy for you.

Thank you. Watch this.

She dives under the water and does a leaning handstand.

She emerges after an hour, the little hairs on her belly glittering in the glancing sun, lies down on the pool chair next to mine, and announces that she yearns for a child. That is how she puts it. Not wants, *yearns,* like she is the wife in a fairy tale.

Sometimes at night if Bree can't sleep, I tell her fairy tales. I butcher the order of things, confuse this stepsister for that fairy godmother. But I capture the gist—don't be a bitch, don't want too much, or be prepared to suffer.

Look at that fat baby there, Bree is saying. The one with the yellow duck hat. I see her and it's like, *Ow.*

She points to the delightfully domed flesh peeking out between where her halter swim top ends and her suit bottoms begin.

I think we're ready, Bree goes on; she is full-time now, a math teacher at one of Philadelphia's most sought-after public magnet high schools, and my promotion at the museum, a place of great prestige and great hypocrisy, means we'd both be able to take paid parental leave. We'd unfreeze her eggs and find a donor. We wouldn't spend ourselves into the poorhouse, limits would be drawn in all the sensible places, but we'd give it a good college try.

What if it's a boy? I ask.

Back in the sea, she jokes.

What if it's a girl?

Fun, she says. But also, we won't know who they will become. Not for years.

True, I say.

Think about it.

I promise I will and Bree sits up to hug me, which is no easy feat on a plastic pool chair. Behind her head, men in snapbacks down amber-colored beers and the pool glints. A pale white teenaged girl in a pink string bikini stands in the shallow end clutching her own elbows. And then she is there again. Swiffer Girl.

You could make the argument, and you would not be wrong to make it, that sex has been *the* thing that has controlled my life. When Bree and I met, I was coming out of a phase in which whenever I had a bad feeling, I'd abscond to Europe to house-sit and fuck strangers. I was also convinced I was a sex and love addict, and had developed a thing where I could not come during sex without sobbing. I sought the advice of a sex-specific therapist, who was kind and reassuring about it. It is natural in a Judeo-Christian culture for shame and desire to get wound around each other, she said. You are not broken. You are not. But I wasn't sure. I am still not.

The meetings of Sex and Love Addicts Anonymous, SLAA for short, pronounced like the mayonnaisey side dish, were held on the third floor of a church near Rittenhouse Square, in a room that was, otherwise, a children's daycare. There was a single plastic child's stove, seven plastic phones, and seven plastic calculators so kids could practice talking on the phone while doing other things. There was a clock with cats instead of numbers, and seven o'clock, when the meeting began, was an orange tabby. People would gather, and by people I mean men except for a tall butch woman named Gin, and me. The leader, a gay man who wore black jeans—dungarees, my father would have called them—with black clogs and black socks, would read a list of behaviors, most of which I had done at some point or another.

This is a description, the leader would say, not an indictment. He had ten years of sobriety, the precise meaning of which in this context I could not bring myself to ask, even when the floor was open for questions.

One day, we discussed the topic of sexual objectification.

I do it to every woman I look at, said a man with thick hair parted down the middle like a Disney prince.

I get married a hundred times a day in my mind, said another, in an expensive indigo zip-up sweater.

A tall man whose legs, when crossed, wrapped an extra

time around each other and who started in the group on the same day I did, said, I have been reading the big green book and in there it says that objectification is harm. I did it on my way here. I passed a woman in my car and then I watched her walk away in my rearview mirror, and when I couldn't see her anymore I stuck my head out the window and watched her with my head turned. That is spiritual harm to her which I have done, of which I am guilty, and which is wrong. So now I will say a prayer. I will say, Sister, may no harm come to you from my thoughts or actions. Sister, may you be free.

A short man, a teacher who was visiting from a different meeting and had talked in the break about the carrots he was growing in his backyard, spoke then. I am trying so hard, he said, not to do it to my daughter. Not to harm her body with my eyes.

The room was silent.

A helpful tool, said the leader, is the three-second rule. You can look for three seconds, but then you look away.

For a time, I tried to put these principles into practice. Leaving the meetings, Gin would stand up and put on her jean jacket and there would be a rolling, a feeling of ignition, something deep and almost cellular in my middle section that would tip and then flip over. But instead of watching her walk the room's full length, noting the way her collar held stiff and her hair was buzzed behind her ears, I would look as she stood up and then look away. I would keep my eyes down.

You might be a sex and love addict, my therapist said at some point that season, but if that is the case, then so is every person in this world.

. . .

When we get home from the pool, Bree takes off all her clothes and, still in her damp swimsuit, settles into the couch to read a book about seed bombs. She has big plans for this summer, which include daily bike rides to a community garden near us in South Philadelphia, sprinkling thousands of flower seeds along the way. I'm going to be like the Lupine Lady from that children's book, she says. She feels a real responsibility, or maybe just a frank desire, to make the world more beautiful.

No shower? I ask. You'll get a UTI.

I will, she says, but not yet. I'm savoring that pool.

I go upstairs to change but when I pass the open doorway of my office there is my computer with its dark, shiny screen.

What happened to Swiffer Girl? *I heard she moved to Texas,* writes one commenter on Reddit. There is a column on a disreputable New York gossip site where a socialite with a vague connection to Lindsay Lohan is quoted as saying that Swiffer Girl opened a Jell-O wrestling club in New Jersey. There is an essay by a literary writer that recounts her stay at a fringe somatic healing camp in Pennsylvania Amish country, claiming that Swiffer Girl had been at the camp too, recovering from a coke habit. There is an obituary online for an Emily Cohen whose parents and brother have the same first names as Swiffer Girl's parents and brother. Someone has left a comment on the "guestbook" of the obituary site that reads *Burn in hell slut.* There must be about a thousand Emily Cohens in America, which is perhaps the only kindness in this whole situation.

She could only have happened where and when she happened, in the Manhattan of the early 2000s when my block still had the gay bookstore/video store/coffee shop and the man with the parrot who spent all day in the sun, before the Pinkberry moved in with its many handles of soft serve and the pottery studio came and hung its red sign. Technically, she was the Bronx, since she originated there, on the strange green campus of one of its ritzy private schools. She was not Brooklyn: the place my father had come from and to which he vowed never to return. It's possible that she reached Queens.

She did it for a guy, I heard at the time, just some guy. And then instead of keeping the video for himself, the guy sent it to all his friends. I recall an email with many, many names, one of those emails that you forward on lest you have bad luck for seven years. The guy faded immediately from view; Swiffer Girl lingered. She was *a crazy whore,* went the comments at school, analog only, for YouTube hadn't yet been invented. Swiffer Girl was *fucking crazy, fucking bitch, whoring bitch, crazy bitch, crazy crazy crazy.*

There had been some discussion at the time about the mechanics of the video's filming, especially given the fact that the ending was so abrupt. Had the camera stopped recording by some sort of accident? Had she kept going to orgasm but edited that part out, wanting to keep it private, just for herself? And who had been standing there behind the camera—a friend? Some other boy, a "nice guy" she didn't love like she loved the one for whom she'd made the video?

Swiffer Girl was my same year, a freshman, and my fancy uptown school was like hers, but a little bit worse. We could have been at the same parties, had I gone to any. The motto of my school was "Go forth unafraid," and the motto of her school was "Warriors ever brave and loyal, making right prevail."

I rode three trains every morning to get to this school, and on each I could expect to see at least one person in mortal danger. A very thin woman in very expensive shoes would be crying in her seat and the woman standing above her in a sweatshirt would be trying not to notice. In the passageway where people ran toward the number 7 train, a man with plastic bags wrapped around his feet would be begging for mercy. There was no time for his mercy, the running people said, their hair streaming behind them, no space in their bodies for what such mercy would require. I was one of them and there was no space in my body either. If you opened yourself up just a smidge, went the thinking, there was no telling what might come rushing in.

This was during the era when *New York* magazine was routinely publishing articles about the dangers children like me were supposedly facing: excessively heavy backpacks that could lead to scoliosis, hookup culture, a college application environment so stressful it was causing nervous breakdowns. There was the constant sense that we were supposed to be busy becoming something great, that we were not just children playing in the dirt but cosmopolitan pre-adults destined to distinguish ourselves in some highly specific way—mastering the cello or learning American Sign Language or showing our youthful designs at the Fashion Institute of Technology. We were supposed to identify the very core of who we were on the inside and then express that core on the outside. It's taken me twenty years to deprogram myself from believing in my potential. None of us, it turns out, were special.

My freshman-year history teacher knew this, which meant she sat alone in the teachers' lounge and students parted around her in the hallway as she walked. She was a fat dyke—though I didn't know this then—who wore a Mets cap over her dark hair.

Lazy, she would say of my essays. Facile, reductive, that's not how it happened at all.

But she loved me back. Oh, how she loved me. She let me stay in the teachers' lounge all through lunch and sometimes into the next period, saying nothing as I watched her read the newspaper and tear through her roast beef sandwich—kaiser roll, mustard, lettuce, no tomato. She ate that sandwich. I ate her.

On each leg of my train journey to school, I could also expect at least one penis—here a flaccid one protruding crookedly through a half-zippered fly by the trash can where I went to throw away my donut wrapper, there an erect one gripped by the hand of a man in a trench coat seated near the conductor's booth. One afternoon, doing the trip in reverse, I nodded off and woke up to a white man in a black suit sitting next to me, his hand on my knee. I regarded the hand and the dark hairs on his knuckles as he squeezed and released my plump kneecap. I sat that way, statue still and hardly breathing, from Forty-Second Street to Twenty-Third, where he stood and exited the car. At home, as at school, I told no one. I thought about telling my history teacher, but then she flexed her muscled arms beneath her T-shirt and I knew she would not understand the thing inside me that made me so weak and such a coward.

My sister Tess was a few grades ahead of me at our school.

Head up, shoulders back, don't scuff your feet, she told me when our lines passed each other in fire drills. She had a boyfriend, a tall boy with a crown of Jewish curls, who trotted the halls with the entitlement of a prizewinning dog. My sister stayed most weekends at his house.

What's wrong with our house? my mother often asked. But she knew.

For every night after he got home from court, my father would post up at the black-tiled kitchen table, flip the oversized newspaper pages, circle each of his wrists with the middle finger and thumb of his other hand to check for fatness, and drink vodka from the freezer until the ice cubes melted. Thus ensconced, he kept watch over the refrigerator and passed comment on my body. If I wanted a glass of skim milk or a piece of toast, it was necessary to squeeze between the broom closet and the back of my father's chair, triggering him to raise his head and look. I felt my father's awareness of the whooshing sound our old wood-paneled Frigidaire made when I pulled it open, felt my father's eyes on my back, my bumpy ponytail, my butt, my legs, the backs of my ankles. Are you sure you want to eat that? he would ask. Men would like you more if you wore your hair down, because it is sexier. Did you know that if you lifted weights, your arms would become less flabby and more toned?

I did know.

I've told all this to Bree, all my various hurts and darknesses and small slights from childhood, and she has told me all of hers from growing up in West Philadelphia with a brilliant bipolar professor mother and a religious uncle—who told her that the only possible result of desiring a man, let alone a woman, was a thousand years of fire—to her college years at Penn dating rapey white guys. To her, with this history, it is a triumph that she feels desire at all.

We are doing so good, Bree said once. We are asking all the right questions.

When the sky through my high office windows changes from white to gray, I push my chair back from my desk and call Tess. She almost never answers, but today she does, and there is her low voice and the sound of her turning on the squeaky tap in her ancient kitchen.

Tess still lives in New York, a place she can't imagine leaving just as I couldn't imagine staying. She moved to a part of Brooklyn that is less than a mile from the apartment building by the ocean where our father grew up. He wouldn't set foot back in that neighborhood, not even when it got a little bit cool and a newly opened Russian restaurant famous for its floor shows and its free bottle of vodka for every table was written up in *The New York Times.*

Congratulations, she says when I tell her that Bree wants to start trying, and means it; there is real enthusiasm in her voice.

Tess tells me about a bar in her neighborhood, themed

around the movie *Jaws,* that she went to with a woman she is seeing—a tall woman who reviews movies for an internet culture website.

My date couldn't stop staring at a replica of the hot woman who gets eaten by the shark, Tess says. It was so weird. There was fake blood running down the statue's fake perfect ass and legs.

So what did you do? I ask.

We went back to her place and had sex and then I left.

Nice.

It was, she says. She did this thing with her hand, it was like she was tickling my stomach but from the back.

In a good way?

Yes.

Do you think we're fucked-up about sex because of Dad? I ask then.

Of course, Tess says. But show me a woman in America who isn't fucked-up about sex because of her parents. Because it wasn't just Dad, it was Mom too, with her prudery. Weird opposites. No good can come of it.

A pause. Tess turns her tap on and then off again.

Do you remember Swiffer Girl? I ask.

Do I. I dressed up as her one Halloween. I wore the pink bikini and carried the Swiffer around and everything. It snowed and I nearly froze to death on the G train.

But how did she do it? Who filmed it?

She filmed it herself. Apparently, her dad was in like tech sales and got a special camera for her? It had a remote control.

Oh.

Yeah. Sad, huh.

Too sad, I say. I don't like that story.

How about a sister? she says. Whenever I tell the story of Swiffer Girl at parties, I always add a sister.

You do? I say, and I feel fifty percent less alone in the world.

Yeah, Tess says. Anyway, I heard she's like a Mormon now. Very religious.

When I was in college, I could always tell when I was going to get blackout drunk. It wasn't a conscious intention; it was a sense of tightness in my chest and a feeling like, *Go go go.* But I was lucky. I chose a small liberal arts college in Portland where there were no frats, only an improv group that threw parties in the basement of the college coffeehouse that also housed an upperclassmen dorm. One night at one such party, I was drinking a glass of straight Popov vodka through a green bendy straw. The next thing I knew I was in one of the upstairs dorm rooms with one of the guys from the improv group, wearing nothing but an oversized T-shirt and some underwear. Things were now very clear, as if I had been shaken awake from a dream. There was no hazy coming to, it was harsh and happening. The guy kept trying to take my underwear off, and I kept trying to put it back on.

Whose underwear is this? I said when the guy had taken it off me once again. It was hot pink and sort of stringy.

It's yours, he said, perplexed.

No, I said, you're lying.

We went back and forth like that until I got up and left his room and went into the hallway. He took my hands and asked me to sit down, to wait. And then I was crouching on the floor of the dorm's hallway screaming at this guy. I was screaming at him to get away from me and also to give me my underwear back. It was such a strange moment because I was both totally drunk and totally lucid, a way of being that moves you through space and time. Eventually, the guy brought me my clothes and went to sleep in his room. I stayed out there in the hallway a long time.

That may have been the first time since the day I watched the video that I really remembered her—Swiffer Girl.

I remember that the day I watched the video was in early spring and that it was after school, in that swath of unsupervised afternoon when my parents were both still at work and my sister was at Model United Nations club rhetorically murdering the less intellectually fortunate.

I watched the video all alone in the small room next to my bedroom. The room contained only a couch, a big double window, stacked vertically, that looked out onto the roof of the Irish bar next door, and a garishly colored computer with a back made of clear plastic so you could see the machine's workings. This was before there were smartphones for the masses but after AOL, in that brief sliver of years when we knew what the internet was but did not yet know what it meant.

After watching the video, I took the elevator down to the lobby. Someone had scratched the initials KR into the elevator panel just below the emergency button and the whole car smelled of sweet Cuban cigars from the man in 7G. His wife wouldn't let him light up in the apartment, so he rode the elevator up and down, sometimes all night, pressing buttons and smoking.

Every pump at the gas station across the avenue from our apartment building was full at four o'clock, drivers shouting greetings at each other over the hoods of their cabs. I was a child and I had no parents and no sister and no best friend, but I had my own set of keys to our apartment and I had these cabdrivers and the sun on my neck beneath my ponytail. I had this city. There was still garbage in every gutter and the streets still had room for me.

At Anna's Deli on the corner, I perused the slices of cut melon in clear plastic containers rubber-banded closed and stamped $1.99, as well as the pieces of cake wrapped in Saran Wrap and piled in the plastic basket by the register. I ran my hand over the 24-hour energy drinks, the penis-enlargement pills, the discounted bagels with butter, but bought nothing.

From Anna's, I drifted to the gay bookstore/video store/coffee shop where two men in muscle tees were staring deeply into each other's eyes over cups of coffee as big as bowls.

My mother was an actress, the taller one said. Very glamorous, huge tits, huge hair. I'd watch her getting ready to go out.

Really? the shorter one said.

Really.

I wondered if this was how it was accomplished—sex, and maybe even love—and if this couple would end up together forever. I knew about gay men and saw them all the time, but I wouldn't know the word *lesbian* until years later. I definitely heard it in high school, but somehow I never saw it, and certainly never believed in it.

The shorter one noticed me first, as I was standing in front of their table, staring openly.

You OK, sweetie? he said.

Other people at other tables, some men browsing the books and videos arranged along the walls, the barista, and the man who had brought his parrot inside with him all turned their heads to look at me. Looking, looking, always there was looking. I turned and ran very fast down the block back to our apartment where I dragged the video of Swiffer Girl to my computer's trash and emptied it.

There is one other video that needs to be discussed, even though I'd rather not discuss it. It was a video I downloaded on the same computer where I watched the video of Swiffer Girl, through a service where you could illegally download music and porn. I watched this video about a year after I watched Swiffer Girl for the first time, though I would return to watch it many times.

I don't remember selecting the video or even seeing a thumbnail of its content, nothing like now where you can search and filter, only that I wanted to watch sex and this was the sex I got. In the video, a lean older man and a young teenaged girl dressed in a schoolgirl skirt are standing in front of the hatchback trunk of a square station wagon, the wagon's door lifted in the air. The man pushes the girl into the car and starts to undress her. No, Daddy, she is saying. It's OK, sweetie, be a good girl, the man is saying. The implication, though now I am not sure how exactly I knew this was the implication, was that "Daddy" was not a sexy term of power play but a descriptor of reality; this male actor was meant to be playing the female actor's father. In the video, the man pulls off the girl's underwear and then fucks her from behind, but also sort of on his side. What I remember is that the man kept his T-shirt on while the girl was fully naked and that the man's balls, which were long and stretched out, got very red from all that effort.

Here are three additional true things about this video: 1) It was less than three minutes long; 2) I must have watched it thirty or forty times between the ages of fourteen and eighteen; and 3) It was lost sometime around college when they cracked down on illegal file sharing, so I will never know if what I remember about it is true or feel sure that it ever even existed at all.

Now that I'm older, I know that these facts don't mean I actually wanted to have sex with my father, and I know that my father worried he *was* sex, just as I now worry *I* am. What happens to make sex huge, a force that can hijack a life, catapult it up into the air then slam it back down again, is a question I have often asked myself. But the answer is: anything. Anything at all.

. . .

It takes hours of sitting in my office and clicking through archived torrented videos, but I eventually find Swiffer Girl again. Just as I suspected, nothing on the internet, least of all a video of a girl, ever truly dies.

As I watch, I pause the video several times and bring my face very close to the screen to examine the texture of the Swiffer's handle. It looks plastic, rough, almost corrugated. But in a good way?

Swiffer Girl's face on the screen is not exactly a face, but more like the back of a dinner plate—smooth and white and full of light, yet somehow turned away. She had the good sense not to be completely naked, to wear that pink string bikini. But when the camera zooms out, I can see her whole stomach, very pale, and then the top of her vagina area, boring with its few wisps. She holds up the butt of the Swiffer pole and fellates it in a perfunctory way for several minutes, then gets on all fours and inserts it into what I thought when I first watched it was her butt but which is definitely not her butt. She mostly keeps her right palm down on the bedsheets (gray, cotton, no pattern) and keeps the pole steady with her left hand. She keeps bringing her body onto it; the Swiffer handle keeps going in and out. Her hair, which is curly but which she clearly had chemically straightened, falls in sharp pieces into her eyes and when she can take it no longer she sits back on her knees and brushes the hair away with her whole hand. I can see that the curls at her forehead have reverted to their natural texture. She looks at the camera. Her eyes stay open. Her mouth stays closed. The video is soundless except for the sound of the actual Swiffer part, the part you would use to clean, sort of flopping around on the bed behind her. It hits the sheet with its wide, almost sharp side over and over again.

It is dark now, the gloaming, I guess you would call it, and people are walking down the sidewalks of our wide street; I can see them from my window. It's Saturday night and they are going places. Maybe after we eat noodles, Bree and I will go for water ice at the place a few blocks away that is basically just someone's house. Whenever you go there you have to ring the doorbell and a mother and daughter come out. The mother scoops your water ice and it is tart and zingy, which is a word that my father loved just because it is fun to say. The little girl takes your money.

Hannah? Bree calls through my closed door and I startle, hit the keyboard. Swiffer Girl is still on my screen.

Yeah? I call back.

But there's no answer.

Yeah? I call again, opening the door. For a moment, I'm convinced that Bree knows what I've been up to and is going to leave me.

I hear the water running and follow it into our bathroom and Bree is standing in the glassed-in shower washing her legs, still in her bathing suit, and humming a jaunty tune.

She says something I can't hear.

What? I say.

Come in, Bree says. She presses her stomach to the glass. She spreads her arms wide.

I will, I say, speaking in the future tense.

The New York City where I grew up is gone. Many places all over the world are gone, so why should the ones that meant something to me be any exception? But there is a particular speed at which that place turns over, erases itself and regenerates. There's a glass-and-chrome apartment building with a nail salon on the ground floor where the gay bookstore/video store/coffee shop used to be. Anna's Deli is now a high-end lingerie store. My father is dead.

Come on in and join me, Bree says again. She moves her arms up and down the glass, like she's making a snow angel.

Have a daughter, Swiffer Girl says to me, from Texas, maybe. That's the scenario I'm hoping for, that she lives far away from where we started, in a little house in the part of Texas they call Hill Country. It's not so bad, she says, clothed now in sweats and on the porch of her little house, iced tea in hand. Of course it's very bad, she says. But we survived it.

I take off my T-shirt and shorts and press my bare stomach to the glass too, which makes a satisfying squelching noise. I try to line my body up with Bree's, though she is bigger and taller. When she moves her arms I find I'm able to follow, to mirror her, to fake it until I make it, like I am scrubbing my side of the glass clean or making my own personal kind of swimming.

CAMP SENSATION

Perhaps you are sick and fear you will never be well, the brochure said, more or less. Perhaps you spend your days off on the couch, half napping, half awake. Perhaps your thighs, stomach, feet, and arms have become not so much *you* but accessories to you, things to hold and prod. If any of this sounds familiar, the brochure said, Camp Sensation may be for you.

Cara noticed the brochure one Sunday morning, as she stood in line at the organic foods co-op in her neighborhood. The store had four checkout stations arranged in a square and the line formed down the bulletin board wall. It held the usual posters and business cards, all familiar to Cara because she'd used many of their services already—massage therapists and life coaches and expensive eating-disorder-informed-health-at-every-size nutritionists and queer-affirming couples therapists and a shaman that promised to inoculate a body against the allergens of a specific cat using a tuft of its fur. But unlike these others, which were all just text printed on matte blue or white Xerox paper, the brochure for Camp Sensation was glossy and professionally tri-folded.

Cara put down her shopping basket and read the front of the brochure, then flipped it over.

For all of Cara's life, an air-conditioning unit had been running at the back of her brain. It made a groaning noise when it was on, a sound that conveyed a message: *Instead of living cells, your body is made of decaying matter; your flesh is rancid chicken breasts and your blood is trash juice.*

The air conditioner wheezed with age, cycling on and off. Sometimes, such as when Cara had had to buy a bridesmaid's dress for a wedding and the salon asked her if she'd like to wait until she was no longer at her "winter weight," or when she visited her mother in Reading, the fan seemed clogged and the air conditioner's message screamed louder. Sometimes, such as when Cara was seeing the expensive nutritionist regularly, or lifting weights, the air-conditioning unit hummed along quietly, as if the parts had been recently cleaned. But never did it turn off completely.

Next shopper! the cashier called.

The cashier's long blond hair hung down into Cara's produce as he struggled with the keys of the cash register, *boop-boop*ing around until eventually striking the right one.

What a truly magnificent smell, he said, lifting Cara's selected bag of lemons to his nose and inhaling dramatically. Is there anything better in the world than the smell of citrus?

Cara hadn't thought to smell the waxy yellow fruits. As the cashier tenderly rolled the lemons into a used paper bag, Cara found that the brochure for Camp Sensation was still in her hand.

. . .

It was ten days. One day for each of the five senses, and five more days—for what exactly?

There are some things we cannot explain over the phone, the woman who answered the number on the brochure told Cara.

In the absence of an explanation, Cara memorized every line of the brochure as she sat in her cubicle at the Philadelphia Department of Health. Things were slow that summer and Cara had the necessary days saved as well as professional development money to use or lose. Every time she thought she might use it, some catastrophe was visited upon the city—rates of chlamydia spiked and the mayor wanted an immediate explanation; some senator in Harrisburg learned the phrase *childhood obesity* and wouldn't shut up about it.

Cara hired a cat-sitter. She packed a suitcase. She took the photograph of her as a baby wearing a teal tutu that she kept on her fridge at the expensive nutritionist's insistence to remind her that she had once been a child worthy of feeding.

She brought her wandering Jew and jade plants over to her best friend Jules's apartment.

A therapeutic retreat, she told him.

It sounds weird, Jules said, assembling the ingredients for a kale smoothie. In a good way, he said. The way artist residencies are weird.

Before taking her current job, Cara had tried to be an artist, dropping out of a master's program for sculpture at the State University only to enroll a few years later at the City

University for creative writing. In between and simultaneously, she'd also been: a suicide crisis center operator, a bread baker, a housemate to many housemates, a girlfriend to a polyamorous hot commodity around Philadelphia who had taken her to see ponies, and a flaky volunteer/disorganized activist for organizations and causes ranging from high school students organizing against the school-to-prison pipeline to a halfway house for trans women. "Essayist" had been the most recent personality she'd tried on, thinking perhaps it would finally let her knit together all these disparate strands with the common thread of her mind, but she'd written little more than emails since graduating. Jules knew all this and had been around for much of it.

Good for you, he said now. Just make sure to come back.

Haha, Cara said.

The real air conditioner in Jules's apartment cycled on.

The July day that Cara left for Camp Sensation was bright and jangling with sounds that moved too quickly through her ears. Cara pulled her Toyota away from the uneven curb in front of the Victorian that housed her first-floor apartment and headed west and north, following a tree-named street until it dead-ended at the city limit and curved up into a four-lane roadway. The suburban Saturday morning road was clogged with gleaming luxury car dealerships and red Wawa signs and people in a hurry to recreate. Cara passed the brick entrance to the small college she'd attended as an undergraduate, a place where she had glugged, blacked out, loved and been loved, and rolled down soft green hills, ultimately cracking the papier-mâché shell that had held her in childhood. Once cracked, everything had rushed in—pleasure and friendship and injustice and what it meant to be accountable to other people. Also, she'd first seen a therapist there because it was free, started eating solid food every day, and doubled her body weight.

The road divided and a grassy median rose, separating Cara's car from traffic going the other way. Cara felt the tightness in her chest and in her grip on the wheel loosen. It was a straight shot now, just two hours. Her foot on the gas pedal felt light and heavy at the same time. Driving—moving all these pounds of metal to get where we are going—seemed like it came from the mind alone. But, Cara knew, it did not.

Soon lush trees and gravel quarries lined the road which climbed steadily, opening views of green hills and dry yellow fields. Cara passed a diner in the shape of a windmill, then a diner in the shape of a UFO. The road narrowed into a two-lane and SUVs and campers barreled toward and then away from her. She passed cows and horses clustering beneath the shade of single trees and saw her first buggy, a black top with two figures inside it. The man was seated on the right holding the reins and the woman on the left, closer to Cara. As Cara passed them, the woman turned her face away and covered it with her hand.

Just before Lancaster at an intersection where an Amish family was selling whoopie pies, she turned off the main road per the instructions she'd been given. GPS and Google Maps are not accurate in our area, the brochure had said. If you pass the Amish feedstore, you've gone too far. The road was still paved but more roughly; big lumps of tar pooled on the shaggy edges where the asphalt had worn away. To each side was red dirt and wide fields of swaying corn.

Cara pulled into the feedstore's parking lot and turned around, retracing her route back to the main road, but still she did not find Camp Sensation. The second time, she went past the feedstore just in case, only to end up at a small gas station where she got out to chase a bar of reception.

A man in a navy blue baseball cap pumping gas into a maroon SUV looked her body up and down.

You looking for that health camp? he said.

Cara nodded.

Good for you, the guy said. I used to be fat. You wouldn't know it to look at me now but I was.

Oh, Cara said. That's not—

You've got to pay attention, the man said. When you feel the trees change from evergreen to deciduous, that's them.

Driving slower now, Cara eventually found it—a clump of kudzu concealed a small dirt road with a woodburned sign that read CAMP SENSATION. Trees leaned toward each other, their low branches touching the hood of Cara's car as it plowed forward. But the guy had been right: the plants did change. All the trees on this road seemed brighter, lighter, dusted with the opaque coating of grapes at the grocery store. Cara wanted a grape then, green and very taut, craved the sensation of putting one in her mouth and puncturing its hard skin with her teeth. The air smelled like sulfur.

The terrain became rockier and Cara's car jostled, the underside scraping badly as the road continued for several miles. A mist rolled in, then became denser, settling on the windshield of Cara's car, the kind of wet fog that suggested being close to an ocean, though she was not. Cara rolled down her window and stuck her arm out; it came back wet. She ran an index finger along her forearm. Licked it: salty.

The road curved to the left suddenly and steeply and up the car went, groaning, momentarily spinning out. Cara slowed and applied gentle pressure to the accelerator; she was a country girl after all, and remembered how. At the top of the hill, the fog was so dense that the windshield was simply white. She stopped the car and got out; underneath her feet now was a fine gravel—sharp and pale.

In the near distance, a bright yellow light rotated, emitting a powerful beam. Cara walked slowly on, crunching over the gravel toward the light until she reached a circular stone building with a domed roof. She knocked at its glass-paned front door.

Welcome welcome, said a woman—very tan, in her sixties, with the ropy muscles of a thru hiker, white hair swept up enviably in an Anne of Green Gables–style pouf—who showed Cara into a vaulted great room. A fire burned in the fireplace, tended by a little boy in a red sweatshirt, and the room had a grand wood dining table and oversized French doors, which provided relief from the heavy dankness of all the stone.

Crazy weather we're having, said the woman, whose name was actually Anne. Perhaps Cara had sensed it.

These valleys have a kind of microclimate all their own,

she went on. I do apologize that the road isn't better marked, that's on the list.

On my list, you mean, said the little boy, who was perhaps neither so little nor a boy.

Meet my grandchild, Lou, Anne said. They help me run this place in the summers when they're home from college.

Lou pushed back the hood of their sweatshirt, revealing a round, pimpled face, gauged earlobes, and long middle-parted brown hair. They rested their hands on their big belly inside the hoodie's pouch.

It's true, Lou said. Plus, I have ideas of my own. I won a prize from the physics department.

What for? Cara asked.

That's personal, Lou said.

Propped up on the dining room table was a board with a map of the Camp Sensation property. Dense stamps of crude green triangles stood in for forestland, Anne explained; black circles for structures, and brown lines for roads, such as they were. Sight, Hearing, Smell, Touch, and Taste were the names of the five cottages. It was an exclusive experience, only five participants at a time.

You'll be in Touch, Anne said.

I'm in charge of the sauna, Lou said, if you're into that.

Back in Philadelphia, on March days when winter had lodged itself so far down in her bones that the prospect of her big naked body being gawked at by tiny aunties felt worth it, Cara sometimes went to the affordable Korean spa. But the sauna with its dry wall of heat from which there was no relief was her last choice, only on the menu if the jade room and steam rooms were stuffed to bursting.

Anne gave Lou a sharp look and Lou turned back to poke the fire.

I'll think about it, Cara said.

Anne followed Cara to the trunk of her car, took up her heaviest backpack, then led the way off into the mist. They walked over a grassy field, squishy from rain.

This your place? Cara asked. You're the owner?

I suppose I am, Anne said. Ever since my husband died. He was fifth-generation in these mountains, grew up Amish, knew every inch of this property. I moved here in the seventies to go back to the land—dropping out, counterculture, making my own bread, washing my own clothes, and all that. We fell in love, so I stayed.

He left the community to marry you?

He did, Anne said. It wasn't easy. He missed his family, who he couldn't see, even though they only lived over the next hillside. So he brought them into this place by building things the way they would have built them, keeping some of the traditions alive. That's why there's no screens here, or internet. And the religion, in his way. There's still his little church, or singing place, on the property—or was, until Lou turned it into the sauna.

The path narrowed and tall lacy ferns rose on both sides. They passed a grand firepit with benches constructed from thin branches. Beyond this, a stand of trees, and an oval lake whose wide edges were dotted with small round stone cottages. This lake was not the dark blue-black color of most lakes, but rather light, reflective, nearly aquamarine.

You can swim if you wish, Anne said.

That's OK, Cara said. I didn't bring a suit.

Too bad, Anne said. It was on the packing list.

Cara liked neither to be wet nor all the logistics involved in swimming—the pulling on of the suit that always seemed to stretch and be rigid in all the wrong places. She didn't like the getting in, especially when it involved a marshy entrance strategy, the squish of toes against a warm yet unknown soft substrate. She didn't like the being in, the way the water surrounded her skin and beaded on it when she emerged, nor did she like the slow process of drying off after water immersion, the hours of moistness, skin rubbing against other skin until it was macerated.

Anne stopped in front of one of the stone cottages, which featured a door as small and rounded as a hobbit's and above which the word TOUCH had been burned into a piece of wood. Anne bent over to enter and Cara followed. Inside, the ceiling was higher and it was easier to stand, but cold. There was a fireplace and plenty of wood.

Out one of her small arched windows, Cara saw a person—masculine but not a man—sitting on a bench outside the closest cottage, marked SIGHT. She was white and long-limbed, with rosacea on her upper arms, short hair tucked beneath a beanie. Her feet were sheathed in hiking boots too stiff and clean to have ever been worn before.

Dinner lasts until nine, Anne was saying. We encourage

you to listen to your body and come when it tells you that you are hungry.

What if I can't tell? Cara had said this many times before, to many medical professionals, but none had offered such a direct answer as Anne did then.

Try, said Anne.

Cara tried. She sat down on the bed, which was somehow soft and firm at the same time. The comforter was light, almost freakishly so, but with a thick, warm appearance. She unpacked the pillow she'd brought, though it seemed lumpy and false now in comparison to the fluffed and elegant offering that came with the cottage. She put her book on the bedside table and opened it to the photograph of herself as a baby. She wondered what Jules was up to. Probably working out. Jules loved to work out. He wrote down how much weight he could lift in a certain move called a "clean and jerk" in a small notebook that he carried in the back pocket of his jeans. Perhaps Cara should try it.

Don't bother, said the air-conditioning unit in her mind. That day, it was very loud. Cara pressed her fingers into her stomach so she could feel the air going into and coming out of it. She lifted her breasts and felt around under them. Through the substantial layer of fat she thought she could feel where her rib cage ended and the other stuff began. She could feel her lower back, which had started hurting recently since she began sleeping on her stomach with one leg up.

She could feel an itch on the outer labia of her vagina, which according to the internet might be a small patch of eczema, a bit of skin that had grown abnormally thick from her scratching at it at night—*lichenification,* an article had called it. Cara thought of the lichen that was surely growing on the rocks surrounding the Camp Sensation lake. What was an itch, anyway? Cara tried to look it up on her phone but had no reception. No matter, because she had looked up this very question many times before from her cubicle at the Department of Health.

While it can be a nuisance, itching serves as an important sensory and self-protective mechanism, as do other skin sensations such as touch, pain, vibration, cold, and heat, which can alert us to harmful external agents, the internet had said in the past. Despite approximately a century of research, there is no single effective anti-itch treatment.

In other words: unbearable. In other words: bear it.

When Cara retraced her steps to arrive back at the main house for dinner, three other guests were already sitting around the big wood table with Anne and Lou, eating from colorful Fiestaware plates and drinking water from large yellow glass chalices. A place had been set for Cara in the middle of the table.

Chicken? asked Michael/Hearing from his place at her left. All the guests wore nametags with their name and sense, and already, in Cara's mind, their senses were replacing their names. He served Cara, then himself, roast chicken, healthful grains, and butternut squash.

Hearing was white and wide and short, wearing green cargo pants and hiking sandals that were just toes and heels connected by what looked like bungee cords. He had a thick head of brown hair that was going to silver around his ears in a way that drew attention to those sensitive organs.

Cara wondered if this was on purpose, if his sense and indeed all of theirs had been assigned on arrival according to some salient feature, or if the ears were purely synchronicity. Whether the former or the latter, what did it mean that she was assigned Touch? She put down her heavy fork, placed her hands on her thighs, and looked down at them. They were hairy and plump, with chipping blue nail polish left over from her sister's wedding.

At that wedding, a few weeks earlier, Cara had been taking a quiet moment to vape when her sister, June, tipsy on mid-tier champagne, came into the little wainscoted room they'd used to store their purses and flat shoes.

I'm really happy, June said.

I'm glad, Cara said.

I want you to be happy too, June said.

I don't know if we all have to be happy, Cara said. Maybe it's enough just that I am still here.

But come on, June said. Then she burped, a deep yet buoyant champagne burp. Have you tried? June asked. Have you really and truly tried?

I've tried, Cara said, a sharpness rising in her voice. I've tried everything.

Everything? June asked.

. . .

I wonder if there will be hammocks, said Bree/Taste, a tall and large Black woman to Cara's right with hair cropped closely to her skull. She wore a jewel-toned top with sleeves that were slit from the shoulder to the wrist. My partner and I just bought a hammock for our house in South Philly and it's done wonders for my sense of embodiment.

Mmm, said Beatrice/Smell, a very thin and freckled woman whose arms were covered by a layer of white fuzz and whose long blond hair was held back by a pale purple headband. I read an article, she said, about how the swaying of hammocks can reactivate something somatic from the womb.

Gin/Sight, Cara's next-door neighbor, came in late and took the chair across the table. When Sight turned around to accept an offered plate, the shaved hair on the back of her neck formed a suggestive downward V.

What'd I miss? Sight said, helping herself to a hearty spoonful of squash.

We were just discussing children, Hearing said, though they had not. Who here has kids?

Taste smiled but said nothing. Sight rearranged the front of her hair and looked bored. Cara shook her head.

No one? Hearing said. How interesting. He took one sip then another of his water with lemon, the only item he seemed to be genuinely enjoying.

Oh, I do, Smell said, looking up suddenly from her plate. Sometimes it's like I forget. Haha. I have two kids, a boy and a girl.

I only ask, Hearing said, because I am already missing my daughter so much.

Smell smiled and lifted a bite of squash toward Hearing in general agreement.

What's her name? Taste asked.

Alice, Hearing said. He took out his phone. Look, here, a picture.

The phone came to Cara and she looked at the plump white teenager with red curly hair, then passed it on to Taste.

Taste looked at the photo a long time, even zooming in with her thumb and index finger.

Oh! Taste cried out suddenly, and seemed about to say something else, when Smell, looking at the photo over Taste's shoulder, interrupted her.

Cute, Smell said. But that hair! What a nightmare to brush. Yes yes, I have pictures of my kids around here somewhere. Though you could say my job is kind of my baby. I'm an entrepreneur, started a company with my friend, which has basically taken over my life—you know how it is.

The table paused thoughtfully, no one apparently knowing how it was.

Ah, Hearing said eventually. So it's you I'll have to compete with for the phone.

Actually, Anne said, we discourage you from using the phone during your stay. As you've seen, you won't get reception on your cells. We have a landline, of course, for emergencies, in the kitchen, but we've found over the years that immersing yourself in the experience without contact with your home lives provides the best results.

Oh, Smell said. Oh really? Oh wow.

I'm never having kids, Sight said.

And why not, if I may ask? Hearing said.

Look around you, Sight said. The polar ice caps have melted. In ten years, Manhattan will be underwater. The wind and the rain. The water that will rise. The heat that will kill. Not to mention the patriarchy, educational inequality based solely on class and race and geography, and intergenerational trauma.

Isn't that the truth, Taste said.

Cara nodded, too.

Plus, Sight continued, I have zero interest in becoming pregnant. Think about it for a moment, will you? To become the host to a parasitic being that steals your nutrients, makes itself at home inside your uterus, then ruins your cunt on the way out? No thank you.

Smell made a small, strangled noise. It's true, she whispered. Ever since I had my kids, I barely recognize myself.

But that's what's so magical about it! Hearing said. The body changes. Not mine, obviously, but my ex-wife's. So wild, so animalistic.

I would have liked to have a child, Taste said. My partner and I. We tried. Several times. But in the end, no. We were up against a lot, being gay and me being Black, and my weight. After a while, we just got tired of fighting the system. Plus the hormones, which were very hard. That's kind of why I'm here, actually.

But what I would like to know, Hearing went on, is what do you do with all your healing if you don't have kids? Like, we're all here to work on our relationships with our bodies, right? And I couldn't do it just for myself, but my daughter told me I had to do it. She was like, *Go work on your body stuff, Dad,* and I was like *Why* and she was like *Because it doesn't just affect you, it affects me too.*

Yeah, well, Lou said. Some people just make it worse. Some older people see younger people with less body stuff and they just want to shit all over them.

Wow! Anne said. What a stimulating discussion! What a group! I'm so glad these ideas have surfaced already, for they are exactly what we are here to explore. If you'll take care of your plates in the kitchen and then join me in the parlor for tea, I'll provide a road map for the rest of our time together.

Cara took a seat on the elegant but worn couch next to Smell. Smell lived in a wealthy Philly suburb and had heard about Camp Sensation from her business partner, with whom she ran a wildly successful beauty startup that made the tinted eyebrow gel that Cara was currently wearing.

There's the mom thing, which is its own body trip, Smell said, clinking her spoon against the side of her teacup, plus the drinking a bottle of wine a day thing.

On a site visit to a supplier, Smell told Cara, she had met, and then taken home, a potbellied pig. Smell had apparently taken to massaging the pig's head each night while she watched TV. Her husband and children thought it was weird but she didn't care. She sometimes left her bedroom door closed but unlatched so the pig could nose his way in during the night if he became cold.

It was Lyle who made me remember my body, Smell said.

Taste settled herself in a stately leather coach chair in front of a large window, and rested one Teva-ed foot on the knee of her other leg.

I've heard pigs are very perceptive, Taste said. They feel the whole world through their snouts.

Sight and Hearing sat on a loveseat upholstered in a flamingo-patterned fabric. Anne pulled the piano bench closer into the circle of furniture, retrieved her tea, and sat down. Lou was the last to arrive, walking through the swinging butler door from the dining room, steadying it closed, and leaning against the wall.

Sit, Anne directed them.

Naw, Lou said. I'm good here.

Anne turned back to the group. I'm so excited, she began. So so excited. And grateful. For weeks Lou and I have been preparing for your arrival and making all the necessary arrangements. And now here you are! In the flesh.

Branches scraped against the window behind Taste's head and she turned to look.

Tomorrow will be all about taste, Anne said. We will help you to commune with that sensation using various oral stimulations, reflections, and exercises. Taste is a marvelous sense which we do not understand as well as we should, I think.

After that, she continued, smell, as they are related. Then hearing. Then sight. That will be a fun one. Though they all will be very fun, I really shouldn't pick favorites. Then last but definitely not least, touch.

All eyes turned to Cara. She smiled and, inexplicably, gave two thumbs up.

Touch is complex. We will do what we can within the confines of a single day. Then, the second half of the program is a little different. We are here because we are trying to awaken you to the wild opportunity that is the body, that mystery which is given to every human animal to solve. What are the things every human animal possesses, what is the wisdom that originates in your body, and what blocks you from accessing this magic every single day? These are the questions I asked myself twenty years ago when I began Camp Sensation and these are the questions that still guide our practice, though we have refined our answers over many years of experience, and by using the feedback of our participants. If this experience is not working for you, not accomplishing your goals, please do not hesitate to let Lou or me know.

Anne turned to look at Lou in the doorway and they gave a little wave.

They're very nice, Anne said. They don't bite. Except when they're in one of their moods!

Hearing and Smell laughed.

Anne continued. After we cover each of the five senses, the remaining days will be loosely grouped around exploring the nature of a physical sensation that cannot be firmly assigned to any single sense. Hot and cold, for example. Dry and wet, for another. Snapping your fingers. Erotic pleasure. Pain, such as a sunburn. Any questions?

Hearing raised his hand.

How about ice-skating? he said. My daughter is on the hockey team at her school and it would be nice— He stopped himself. Or perhaps more broadly, he said, gliding across a hard surface?

Anne made a thinking face and turned to Lou. Does the cave still have ice?

No, Lou said.

Sorry about that, Anne said. She made a regret face. But, if you want, after this meeting we can go take a look at the basketball court to see if that might fit your needs? I know we have Rollerblades around here somewhere from the movement seminar a few years back.

Sight got up then.

Excuse me, she said, her face pale. I'm not feeling one hundred percent. I gotta go lie down.

Of course, Anne said. We hope you will honor all of your sensations while you are here, energy and fatigue included.

The room paused, watching Sight go.

Was that a sauna I spied? Smell asked after a few beats. I read a very interesting article on the healing properties of heat.

Oh, indeed, Anne said. Lou built the sauna themself and they're very proud of it. We just ask that you don't use it alone. Please find Lou and they'll assist you.

And with that, since there were no more questions, the meeting was adjourned.

In the kitchen, Hearing took his time washing his teacup. Then he turned and reached for the glass Pyrex still on the kitchen table that had held the grains from dinner and began to wash that, too. Steam rose from the frothy suds and his breathing slowed and evened as he washed.

. . .

If nothing moves inside, the Camp Sensation brochure had said. If when you knock, no one is home.

Cara walked home to her stone cottage in the dark. The outlines of tree branches were visible against the black of the sky because, she could see now, they were different kinds of black. Already, her condition was improving.

The path divided and small signs indicated left for Touch, right for Sight.

Psst! called a voice in the dark. Cara!

It was Sight, who lit her face from below with her cellphone. Come over for a minute?

Cara took the path to Sight's cottage, wet plants brushing against her legs. As she approached, Sight's height filled the doorway. Sight wore glasses now—silver and made of vulnerable wire.

Are you alright? Cara asked.

No, Sight said. My skin feels thin. My ears hurt. My tongue is swollen. More importantly, I'm sad. Come in, Sight said. We'll make a fire.

Sight's cottage had plush white carpet and a diagram of a human lung in a matte gold frame hanging from a peg over a small desk. Cara sat by the woodstove while Sight built the fire.

Here, Sight said, handing Cara some newspaper. Tear this into strips.

Cara sniffed the newspaper before she tore it. It smelled like ink and moisture. Sight rubbed two precut shanks of kindling together. The sound was light, almost hollow, and high, like a joke. When Sight lit the match, it felt to Cara like a magician's trick. Sight tossed the match into the pile of paper, and they both watched it catch and spread.

Where do you live? Cara asked.

Cleveland.

So far.

Sight nodded. The only other program like this is in Montana. But I used to live in Philly, so. I'll go and visit an old friend after this.

Cleveland is strange, Sight went on after a moment, not needing Cara's input into the conversation. It's so soft, so plush, so easy. You drive everywhere. You drive to work and then you drive to get beers after work and then you drive to dinner and then you drive home.

Hmm, Cara said. I like driving.

I used to too, Sight said. But now, I don't know. I don't dislike it, I just don't feel it. When my girlfriend touched me, Sight continued, I couldn't feel it. Touch me, I would say. I am, she would say. I started going to clubs, meeting people who would hit me. Hit me, I would say, and they did. I appeared at home with bruises. What is wrong with you? my girlfriend said. I'm moving out, she said.

I'm sorry, Cara said.

Thanks, Sight said.

Spit spit, the fire said. *Reach, crack, explode!*

I think, Cara said, that I can feel when people touch me.

Sight lifted her hand and took Cara's hand, ran her thumb across Cara's knuckles.

Yup, Cara said, not meeting Sight's eyes. I can feel that.

Well, that's something, Sight said, letting Cara's hand go.

After breakfast, Sight, Smell, Taste, Hearing, and Cara slotted their bodies into a wooden picnic table on the patio behind the main building, leaning into mugs of steaming coffee and tea. They all wore sweaters. The grass was wet; moisture seeped through Cara's sneakers and into her socks. Hearing wiped beads of condensation off his anorak. Taste wore bright blue fingerless gloves and had applied eyeshadow. Smell looked rumpled and half awake—her purple headband was gone.

Lou appeared carrying a tray of matte white bowls covered with white fabric. The same fabric cut into strips with raw edges fluttered over their sweatshirted arm.

Lou made these bowls themself, Anne said from her seat at the picnic table. Pottery is excellent for sensual recovery. We recommend it.

Take one, Lou said, putting the fabric strips in the middle of the table. And put it around your eyes like so.

May I? they said to Hearing.

By all means, Hearing said, but he eyed Lou anxiously.

Lou leaned down and adjusted the fabric over Hearing's eyes and ears. Hearing moved forward slightly, but Lou pulled him back, tying the ends in a bow that hung down over Hearing's hair and neck.

Can you see?

A little. More like I can see light but not what anything is in the light.

Cool, Lou said.

You may need to help each other, Anne said, picking up a strip of fabric and gesturing to Smell, who lifted her hair theatrically, as if Anne were about to clasp together the ends of a new and expensive necklace.

Cara tied hers around her own forehead, then turned to help Taste, who had long nails. Sight did her own, without anyone's assistance.

Alright, Lou said. Lou winked at Cara then made a downward pulling motion with their hands. Cara lowered her blindfold.

You will be presented with many tastes, Anne said. It is not your job or perhaps not even in your best interest to try to identify them. Just let the tastes flow over you. Some may be pleasant, others unpleasant. All tastes are part of living.

There was the sound of the bowls being placed on the picnic table and Cara sensed Lou lean over, close to her, then retreat.

You may begin now, Anne said, by reaching for the first sample and putting it in your mouth.

Cara tasted white bread dunked in warm milk, a thing she had not eaten since childhood, when she went to visit her aunt who lived in a big house near Niagara Falls. This aunt was her mother's much older sister, the closest thing she had to a grandparent since all her blood grandparents had died before she was born—two from alcoholism and two from simply refusing to care for their bodies on any basic level. Her aunt had coughed smoker's phlegm into a red Solo cup and tried to protect Cara and her sister from the comments her mother was making about their bodies—*For God's sake, Arlene, give it a rest.*

More bowls followed. Something that tasted like cedar shingles. Something that tasted like strawberry ice cream.

That day's lunch was less formal than dinner had been the night before. Smell's part was cowlicked and her bangs were thick with grease. She stood by the French doors in the dining room and looked through the glass as she demolished a chicken drumstick held in one hand.

Very good, very good, Anne said, touching Smell's shoulder as she bustled by. Honor your appetite.

Cara sat with Hearing, Sight, and Taste at the table. Hearing, too, looked slightly unwashed; his forehead shone bright. He licked sweet potato puree off his fork, tine by tine.

Taste broke the silence. Did anyone else get something that tasted like watery vinegar salad, the kind that you'd eat on Saturdays in a, say, Seventh-Day Adventist religious setting?

Did anyone else, Sight jumped in, get something that tasted like brownies made from a box, left uncovered for a few days?

Cara and Hearing both shook their heads.

That afternoon, they had several hours to rest or explore the property. Index cards with suggested taste-focused activities had been dropped off in their cottages. The index cards said things like, *Chew a piece of grass and find its mois-*

ture and *Suck on an unexpected patch of skin* and *Journal about a time when you tasted something truly extraordinary.*

Cara sat in her cottage, legs crisscross applesauce on the bed, unsure what to do. She had hoped perhaps that Camp Sensation would include more concrete expertise, that they would have brought in a machine, say, that would analyze her flesh and tell her she was perfectly normal, or an expert in Eastern healing practices who would teach a class on how to break down the false binary between body and mind. She loved classes.

There was a knock on the door and for a strange moment Cara felt sure that it would be Lou. But it was not.

Sight looked over Cara's head into the cottage's interior and spoke rapidly.

Sorry to bother you, I thought maybe we could work together this afternoon since we'd already sort of started but no worries if now isn't good.

It's fine, Cara said. It was her turn to build the fire.

Do you think we should, like, taste the ashes or something? Sight asked. That would be unexpected. She placed a finger in the ash, left over from some previous Touch, and licked it.

Cara scrunched up her face. What does it taste like?

Like sand, Taste said. But creamier. Or richer?

Sight had light blue eyes and slightly crooked, crowded teeth. She had tattoos, just single dark blue lines around each of her biceps. She wore a big belt buckle in the shape of a dog's head and Cara imagined how it would feel to unbuckle it.

Well, what are you gonna taste? Sight asked.

I find you very beautiful, Cara said. I would like to taste you.

Cara tasted Sight's mouth, obviously, but also behind her ears and down the trough between her breasts. Sight rubbed Cara's wetness with her fingers and then tasted her fingers, a thing Cara had seen men do in the movies and which icked her, but in this context was not so icky.

What does my vagina taste like? Cara asked. People in books said oysters, salt, fish.

Sight thought for a moment. It tastes like a juice box, I think, Sight said. Apple. Or possibly grape.

At dinner, Smell wore a thick white robe embroidered with the Camp Sensation logo over soft, expensive-looking lounge-wear and was very quiet.

Where'd you get that robe? Taste asked. I love robes. At home I have one with a hood.

Oh, Smell said. Lou gave it to me.

Smell kept smoothing down her hair. The pale purple headband was back, but askew, down much too far over her forehead. She sniffed the green salad and passed it along to Hearing, who took a single leaf of lettuce with his fingers and then passed it to Taste. Taste was the only one who seemed at ease; she ate slowly, chewing every bite. She had a bright yellow flower behind each ear.

The next morning, Smell day, they reassembled at the picnic table and the blindfold and white bowl ritual was repeated, except this time the process wasn't simultaneous but rather staggered, as Anne and Lou had to come around and wave the bowls beneath each participant's nose. Cara knew it was Lou who was waving her bowls because she could smell their Old Spice deodorant and a harsh mouthwash on their breath. Anne, as she had told the group several times, used only organic personal care products.

The first bowl smelled like the smell of Cara's college boyfriend's penis—Dial soap and inner thigh—and his semen—asparagus and bleach. She could hear the other participants choking, too; perhaps someone even leaned over and threw up, as Cara could feel the vibration of someone moving around on the wooden bench and hear a retching sound. Next, Cara smelled the smell of her college campus. She smelled it in the sunshine of the first real day of spring, when it was tradition for the faculty to put out pinwheels in the dark of night so that the students would wake up to a field of color, slowly turning, and she smelled it in the dark, the grass giving off the wet smell of fertilizer as she smoked hookah with the boyfriend and his friends, men she would avoid talking to now but who at the time had seemed OK, even good.

The next day—Hearing day—Smell was missing from the picnic table.

Anne and Lou stood a few paces away on the patio, their heads bent together, speaking to each other in low voices.

The edge of the denim fabric that held Sight's left thigh touched the edge of the stretch-cotton fabric that held Cara's right one.

Penny for your thoughts? Hearing asked Taste, whose hands were clasped on the table.

Taste smiled. I was just thinking, she said. That we were all babies once.

Sure, Sight said. Once we were all new and pure, without sin, etcetera, etcetera.

Right, Taste said. But also we have the same body now that we had when we were born.

Your skin turns over every two months, Cara said.

Yup, Taste said. But the same bones. The same muscles.

Anne and Lou came and took their places at the head of the picnic table. Regrettably, Anne said, Beatrice decided to leave us early.

Too bad, Hearing said.

Do you think she's alright? Taste asked.

Anne paused. I do, she said, I do think so. This kind of work, you know, can be very emotionally taxing, it can bring things back up that you have forgotten for many years or maybe never consciously knew. This is part of the point of doing it, of course, but it can be intense. If you are used to being in your body for perhaps fifteen minutes a day, to be in it for hours straight can be quite a shock.

Sight cast a slanted look down her nose, which Cara caught with the edge of her chin.

This time, the remaining participants were each given large white noise–canceling headphones in addition to blindfolds. At first there was nothing, but then there was something. Cara heard the sound her mother made when she walked down stairs—ball first, then each individual vertebra cracking. Cara heard the sound her cat made when he jumped from floor to windowsill, the readying crouch and then the release and the syncopated landing—first the front two paws, then the back two. She heard the song they played at her middle school graduation, a tinny ballad by a one-hit wonder with orange hair, and she heard the song that had been playing those nights during the summer between high school and college, when she'd driven around in a yellow hatchback with a girl she'd kissed a few times and the girl's boyfriend until eventually parking in the Walmart parking lot—*he takes off her dress now, let me go*. She had a craving—violent, maybe even physical, you might say—to hear that song.

Her headphones were removed. For a long time, she heard only cicadas—a layer of insect sound and then a second layer on top. Then birds were added, calling out from the sky, and the sound of someone walking down a path, crunching shells.

This is very common, Anne's voice said in response to Cara's tears, and from somewhere over Cara's shoulder a tissue appeared.

Cara heard someone—Sight, it sounded like, since it was so close—sobbing quietly, too, then less quietly, and the sound of Hearing doing that thing men do when they want to cry, are crying, but instead choke and clear their throats over and over again.

. . .

If, when you are sexing your sweetheart, you are also watching television, also clipping your nails, also walking down a hallway in your mind with twelve doors on each side but are no longer interested in passing through any of them, the Camp Sensation brochure had said. Already you know, without touching a single knob, what's behind: the same pale sky, your hands on the wheel, straight road and no traffic, cruise control and a lukewarm cup of gas station coffee.

The next morning, the morning of Sight's day, Sight did not appear at breakfast, and still had not appeared by the time the rest of them had finished their oatmeal with blueberries and taken their seats at the picnic table.

Did you see her this morning? Anne inquired of Cara after fifteen minutes had ticked by.

No, Cara said. A lie. But if Sight was not here now and hadn't sent word, she must have her own private reasons, which suddenly seemed to Cara essential to protect. She had seen Sight that morning, sitting on the steps to her cottage and tapping her bare feet on the stones. Sight had given her a sexy faraway smile and they'd waved to each other across the grass.

Hmm, Lou said. I'll go check. They crunched away.

We'll start with something simple, Anne said. Something you've probably done on your own a thousand times.

They were each to rise from the picnic table, sit under a large tree, look up at its canopy, and write down what they saw. Cara picked a cedar tree. It smelled like Christmas—not like the day itself but like the pre-Christmas festivities and bustle.

Why are these kinds of self-improvement camps always in

the woods, Cara wondered? If only we could get away from asphalt and other human beings, goes the logic. It's hard to be an animal in a city. But other city people had bodies, she knew. That was no excuse.

The underside of the branches really did look like arms, Cara observed, or like veins. Nature mimicking the human, the human mimicking nature. Systems for carrying sugar water, systems for carrying blood. The ends of the tree's branches blew green and fluffy.

After dinner, just as Cara was getting the fire going, there was a knock on her door.

It was Sight, wearing a heavy white robe. Where had she gotten that robe? Didn't matter. Come in, Sight.

Where've you been? Cara asked. Since she'd protected Sight's secrets she felt entitled to them.

Oh, here and there, Sight said. Alright, I've been sauna-ing with Lou. Bro time, she said, haha. They have a different take on this whole process than Anne. Less hippie. More radical.

Radical how?

More confrontational, Sight said. Less *Goddess woo woo* and more *What the fuck are you doing?*

Sounds harsh, Cara said.

It is, a bit, Sight said. But sometimes harshness is necessary to create the conditions for change. Or so Lou says.

You know that thing, Cara said once they'd taken off their clothes and the fire was really cracking, where sex is about to happen and you tell yourself, *OK, here we go to the sex destination, saddle up and get ready,* and then you close your eyes and don't open them until it's over?

Sight's eyes were big as they held Cara gently. Yes, Sight said.

What if we didn't do that?

Fine by me. But how?

I don't know, Cara said. Try.

It sort of worked. Cara opened her eyes a couple times, here a peek at Sight's shoulders and back, there a peek at Sight's knees, the knobs of which were round and shiny.

They proceeded. Cara straddled Sight, and Sight took first one then the other of Cara's large pendulous breasts into her mouth. Sight moaned a bit, had gone someplace else, or so it seemed. But then, she stopped sucking. Cara looked down at Sight but Sight did not look up at Cara; she kept her eyes closed.

What is it? Cara said.

I think, Sight said softly, that I don't want to be here.

This place is a lot, Cara said, and got off Sight's lap.

Yes, Sight said. But also I don't want to here, like right now, with you.

Oh, Cara said. She reached for her T-shirt and put it on. She felt like Winnie-the-Pooh in his tiny shirt but no pants.

Sight sat up. I'm sorry. You're like, beautiful, obviously.

Cara made a face like—*Not obvious.*

And sexy and nice and I thought I wanted to be here, Sight went on, you didn't do anything wrong. It's just that, like, I don't want to do this. I don't want to have sex with you. I think maybe I don't want to have sex with anyone for a while.

Sight covered her eyes with her hands. I do this, she said. This is what I do, and have always done. If a beautiful woman wants me, like I could tell you did, I feel like I have to touch her, not for me, but for her. It's like I don't have any will, like I am chosen.

I didn't mean to, Cara said. Want you.

Yeah, yeah, Sight said, I know. I'm saying this is a me problem.

Cara waited but there was nothing more.

OK, Sight said. She stood up and put on her white robe and sneakers. I'm sorry, she said, and then was gone.

Cara lay awake all night. Was Sight an independent actor or somehow there for her, Cara, to teach her a lesson? But what lesson—the physical sensation of rejection, of a current flowing in one direction only to have it reverse course? Her mouth tasted like chocolate pudding. Her room smelled like smoke. There was the sound of someone screaming—an owl? She watched a single ant make the long journey from her shoulder down her arm and then back up to her shoulder again. The wind blew and blew.

In the morning, at the picnic table, Sight was not there.

Lou stood alone now while Anne sat next to Cara, a yellow legal pad open on her lap.

Gin went home, Lou said. So there's that.

Hearing and Taste and Cara looked at each other.

Anne sighed. Gin actually felt she had found enormous clarity in a shorter-than-average time, Anne said. We're happy for her. She seemed in excellent spirits when I spoke to her this morning.

Isn't it interesting, Lou said, looking around the picnic table, that now, this whole group, except for you, Grandma, is fat?

Anne squinted her eyes and smiled a smile with no joy behind it.

Lou, Anne said, we don't comment on people's bodies here.

I was thinking the same thing, Cara said. And she had been. Only the fat ones remained, as if their flesh provided another layer of emotional protection.

It's kind of nice, actually, Taste said. Like, if you're a thin person, keep scrolling. Let us have this space just for us.

It's kind of like a fat camp but more positive, Hearing offered, setting down his lemon water. My ex-wife tried to send my daughter to one of those.

Lou directed Cara and the others to join hands around the picnic table. Lou took Taste's left hand in their right and Anne's right hand in their left. Taste was further joined to Hearing, who was joined across the table to Cara, who was joined to Anne.

Close your eyes, Lou said. Feel the warmth of a human hand, they said.

Lou then directed the group to drop hands and open their palms. There was a rustling as Lou opened what sounded like many plastic bags and circled around the picnic table, leaning into its center. Once, they bumped Cara's shoulder with their own.

Feel the sensation of clay, Lou said, and then Cara did—first dry and hard, then new and moist. There was a slice of bread, it felt like—first soft, then toasted. There was sandpaper and there was silk.

Feel this quilt, Lou said, made by the hands of one hundred old women in Belize, and feel this other quilt made by the hands of one hundred young women in suburban Maryland. Feel the difference in the stitches, Lou said. Feel the difference in the thread. Feel the difference in their intentions. Feel how some of them have hate in their hearts and some of them have love.

Lou, Anne said.

Fair enough, Lou said. You can't feel that yet. But soon.

At the end of lunch, Lou walked around the table offering a wicker basket. Inside were bundles of index cards, each with a hole punched in its corner and joined by a silver ring. *Activity style: solo,* said the top card of the bundle Cara selected. *Materials: none. Location: a patch of moss around your cottage.*

Choose the largest patch of moss you can find and touch it, the second card in the bundle said. Cara touched it. People were always saying moss felt like velvet, but it didn't. It felt rougher to Cara, and thicker, like a substance that had once covered the body of an animal and then been sheared off.

Wait for it to rain, the card said.

Who knew when these cards had been written and what the weather might bring? But what else to do? Cara waited several minutes, and then sure enough she heard drops pattering on the tree canopy above and then felt the rain reach her, lightly at first, then in great plops. A drop temporarily blinded her when she lifted her head to look, so when she saw the figure moving through the foliage out of the corner of her eye, she wasn't sure at first that it was Taste. Cara wiped her eyes on the hem of her T-shirt and sat up. She heard the heavy running feet and the breaking of branches.

Hey! Cara called out.

Taste stopped and looked straight at Cara through the tree trunks. She was wearing a black one-piece bathing suit and chunky white sneakers.

Is it raining? Cara called. Is it raining for you too?

Taste put a palm out to feel. I think so, she called back. But I was already wet, so I can't say for sure.

Taste turned and continued running, pumping her arms.

Take off your clothes and lie back down, the next card instructed. The rain was warm and the moss was scrunchy and clean. Cara took off her T-shirt and shorts and put them on a rock next to her. Over her head, the trees made small adjustments as their leaves got weighed down by rain and then were relieved of their temporary burdens. The water fell on Cara's stomach and thighs, which were pale, goosebumped, and stretchmarked. She lifted the card ring to eye level so she could keep reading.

Every bit of your skin has nerves of pleasure and pain that work in perfect harmony and perfect efficiency, the card said.

The rain became colder and harder.

Ow, Cara said.

Are you uncomfortable? the last card said. *Good, that's normal. That's life. Life is uncomfortable. Your body will be uncomfortable sometimes, even a lot of times. You will want to run from it, but don't. The body's sole purpose isn't pleasure. When you feel pain, you feel scared, you panic. You want to escape from your fear or stay very still so you feel nothing. But bodies break, bodies suffer, there's nothing wrong. You were not meant to feel nothing.*

The rain was hitting Cara now, whipping her like rope. She grabbed her clothes and scuttled into her cottage.

That night, Anne called everyone together for another meeting. Cara took the seat next to Hearing on the couch, while Lou and Taste took the two large armchairs. Anne stood.

Hole! Hearing said loudly. He was sticking a finger into the small moth hole in the elbow of his sweater, enlarging it. Thread! he cried, unraveling it.

Taste wore a sports bra and basketball shorts and a mesh top over the bra, which looked wet, as it was leaving dark spots in the shape of breasts on the mesh.

Have you been swimming? Cara asked.

Not yet, Taste said. I'm working up to it.

Before Cara could inquire further, Anne began to speak.

Tomorrow marks the beginning of the second phase of your work here at Camp Sensation, Anne said. This is the fun part! This is the part you have been waiting for! This is the part that most people remember! Up until now, Lou and I have been guiding you in a broad program of study. A survey, if you will. Now is your moment to seize the reins and tailor the experience to your particular needs. Electives! Special topics! Independent study! Each morning of the remaining five days, Lou and I will arrange bundles of note cards on the picnic table, like the ones you had today, with directions for different experiments you can do to activate a specific sensation, materials required to be picked up in kits in the kitchen, and directions to site-specific practices. You may need to do the experiment alone, or you may need to do it with a partner, or you may need to do it with a certain instructor, either Lou or myself. Meals will be held at the same times, but other than that, everything we have to offer—the main building, your cottage, the grounds, and all our tools—is at your disposal. Unless we are assisting another participant with an experiment, Lou or I will always be in the main building for emergencies or advice. There is a first aid kit in the kitchen below the sink. Questions?

Just one, Taste said.

Shoot, Anne said, taking her glasses off and letting them dangle from their chain.

It is just so clear to me, Taste said, that what we are here for is love. It's not the body at all, is it? It's love.

Let's talk after the meeting, Anne said.

In the morning, the main building was quiet. No one was up yet, it seemed, though the vat of oatmeal was warm and the almonds had been sliced. Just as Anne said, the dining room held neat stacks of ringed index cards, and Cara picked a few up, though none of them appealed. One was designed to explore stickiness, another crunchiness, another the feeling of falling involving a trampoline. Cara was lethargic and her face hurt, the kind of awakeness that feels temporary.

A flash of activity caught Cara's eye then, and a small whoop of joy brushed her ear. She stepped outside and followed the sounds off trail through a thicket of trees until she was reunited with the path that led to the firepit, and eventually to the lake. The lake's color appeared through the trees, an aquamarine that shimmered in the morning light. The sounds grew louder now—someone yelled, someone coughed, someone called out, Hell yeah! *Splash, splash, ca-thunk!*

They were swimming—all four of them, four little heads bobbing in the glassy blue water. Cara trotted faster, jolted awake by this new development. As the trees fell away, Cara saw that a long, narrow wood dock jutted out in a kind of catwalk that ended in a T. Cara stood on the dock and watched as Lou used their big arms to pull themself out of the water and up onto one side of the T, where they flopped side to side to gain purchase and then stood.

Watch this, they called, and Taste, Hearing, and Anne all lifted their hands over their heads and clapped. It was like a strange music video; Cara even heard music somewhere, a beat to which their claps were keeping time.

Lou backed up a few steps on the dock. Then they ran and jumped high into the air, clutching their knees and joining their hands.

Cannonball! Lou called before the smash. Taste and Hearing both closed their eyes as Lou's body made contact with the surface of the water and barreled on through.

Woohoo! Anne called. The straps of her swimsuit were orange, her goggles were green, and she did a little dance in the water in celebration.

It was Taste who first saw Cara and waved.

Cara walked down the dock and stood in the middle of the T at the wood's edge. Sun shone on her legs and into her eyes. She lifted her hand like a visor to look down at them all.

Come on in, Anne said. The water's fine.

That's OK, Cara said. I still don't have a suit.

I didn't either, Hearing said. And I normally hate swimming, but Lou pushed me in.

Was it a push? Lou asked. I would say it was more of a shove.

Haha, Hearing said. Anyway, now that I'm in, it feels amazing.

It's all Bree's fault, Lou said. This was her request.

It's true, Taste said, swishing her arms from side to side in the water. I used to love to swim.

And then what? Lou said. They leaned back to dunk their hair into the water. They wore a black T-shirt that clung to their skin in big air bubbles.

And then? Taste answered. A carefulness set in. It was sort of like I didn't want anything to jostle me. No sudden movements. That kind of thing.

And now? Cara asked, needing very much to know the answer.

Well, Taste said. I'm jostled.

. . .

Hearing ate with a hearty appetite at lunch, slurping his soup and buttering his bread on both sides. Taste sat on the couch in the living room with a smile on her face but didn't come to the table to eat. Anne, too, was absent. Every so often, the kitchen door would rattle, a few plates would clank around, and then the door would latch again.

Cara, Lou said when Cara was waiting to wash her dish at the sink. We've created a custom exercise just for you and Hearing. Meet me in the living room when you're done here.

I'm intrigued, Hearing said, leaning into the wooden dish rack with a little giggle. He looked unwound, blissed out.

The sun over the lake had gone behind a cloud by the time Lou led Hearing and Cara around the path, then directed them to duck under some branches. A warm breeze rippled across the field and the air smelled like smoke.

Lou stopped them in front of the sauna building, climbed the steps, opened the light pine door, and held it for Cara and Hearing to enter. Up went Hearing inside.

Oh, Cara said. I'd rather not, if it's all the same to you.

It isn't, Lou said.

I really don't like being hot, said Cara.

Lou let the door slam, leaving Hearing inside alone.

Cara, Lou said. Something in you brought you here. Because nothing else was working. What if this is the something you have been looking for?

The moment recalled another. When Cara was a kid, her whole class at school had gone to another camp in the woods to eat organic food and bond. There had been trust falls (terrifying) and a zip line (horrifying) but the thing that had nearly ended Cara was the rock climbing wall. A wooden towerlike structure with multicolored rocks nailed willy-nilly to each of its five sides, up which small children attached to ropes scrambled quickly and then bumped down again. It was not that Cara could not start, it was that she got stuck halfway. Up three or four footholds was where the momentum vanished and she looked down and her legs went jiggly. Every step up seemed wrong, every foothold out of reach. The rope attached to her harness pulled her up by the crotch in a disconcerting way. She was the last one to finish and all the children stood on the ground yelling up. Just move your foot to the yellow one, shouted one boy. No, the green one, shouted a girl. Just reach. You got this, someone else said. I don't, Cara said. There was simply no way. It was offensive, actually, that they thought she could do it. You got this, you got this, they kept saying. Eventually, after enough time had passed and their yelling had turned to resentment and then boredom and then hunger, whichever adult was in charge had let her come down. She never did reach the top.

Fine, Cara said now to Lou.

Inside were two small rooms on either side of a door. Lou directed Hearing and Cara to each take a room and change. On the back of the door in Cara's room hung the same white robe bearing the Camp Sensation insignia that Smell and Sight had worn. It was pleasantly plush and—shockingly—in her size: big enough for her to comfortably tie it closed.

Thus costumed, Cara and Hearing followed Lou through the second interior door. The heat was immediate and momentous and so forceful it made Cara's eyes water, though it had no form, no steam, no color. The sauna was shaped like a small curved amphitheater, with three levels of cedar seating and an open space in the middle for a black metal contraption that resembled a woodstove and supported a basket of gray stones.

Take a seat, Lou said, and began to poke the fire. Make yourselves comfortable.

Cara wondered if this meant she and Hearing would have to take their robes off and see each other naked. Perhaps having the same thought, Hearing sat as close to the wall and as far away from Cara as possible. Cara climbed to the second level, but the heat was so unbearable there that she changed her mind and descended again. She lay down and tried to breathe.

The process won't take long, Lou said. Thirty minutes tops.

Cara took shallow breaths, trying not to let the heat in. Lou poured an aluminum pitcher of water over the hot stones, which hissed mightily. Steam began—how, in the absence of water?—to fill the room, first in thin tendrils that danced around Cara's toes before dissipating, and then more thickly. Cara had the sense that more and more of something was being added to the room while nothing was being taken away. When she rubbed her fingers together, the result wasn't thin like water but viscous and slick as lube.

What's in this stuff? Hearing asked through the fog, his voice disembodied now.

Don't worry about it, Lou said. I'll be right back. The door opened, bringing with it a quick respite of cooler air, then closed again.

I am, Hearing said from his side of the room. Worrying about it.

Me too, Cara said.

Cara's feet began to tingle like they did when she'd sat too long on the couch in one position, the cat on her lap preventing her from reaching the remote, the TV having played all the way through her selected show and now offering something algorithmically related. The tingling feeling spread through her knees and thighs. It was a dull, painful feeling, like growing pains or the ache she'd had when she'd pulled her groin while playing ultimate frisbee in college, an injury that had turned the inside of her right thigh black. The tingling spread through her stomach and rose into her chest, like the feeling of a panic attack, a sense that you could breathe and breathe but never rise, never get up and over some hump. Her arms tingled, particularly the soft flesh of her forearms where she still had scars from when she used to, as a teenager, take the dull blade of an eyebrow scissor and rip it across her skin until she achieved skipping, broken lines of blood. The tips of her fingers tingled where she'd picked the skin so savagely that the thumb sides of both index fingers made diagonal lines instead of straight ones. Her neck where she often pinched and pulled the roll of fat there. The place at the nape of her neck just under her hair where a painful bump formed when she hunched too long at her cubicle desk. The very top of her head.

There was silence in the room except for the sound of Hearing breathing and moving around.

Do you feel a tingling? Cara asked.

Yes, Hearing said. In my lower back and in my throat, he said. A few minutes passed. Now, he said, it's everywhere.

Same, Cara said.

The tingling increased in volume, cranking from a six to a nine out of ten. Cara imagined every organ, every drop of blood rising to the surface of her skin like in those videos she liked to watch where a woman took a magnetic wand and waved it over her lacquered nail to make a pretty pattern. Then Cara heard singing—very soft and then very loud.

Do you hear that? Hearing asked, calling out forcefully.

Yes, Cara said.

It was delicate and clear, many voices singing the same notes, no harmony. There was a slight restless energy in the voices, as if some people were jostling their feet while singing or swatting flies away from their faces. The song went up and then down, as if ascending and then descending stairs, and the lyrics were about rest. *There is rest by and by,* the voices sang; *in the beautiful city there is rest by and by.*

The door opened again and then closed, and the singing cut off, replaced by the sound of glass bottles clinking.

I come bearing gifts, Lou said.

I'm so thirsty, Hearing said.

Move, Lou said to Cara, their face appearing then through the fog. Don't freeze, move your arms, move your legs.

Cara complied and then the tingling went up even further, to a ten. She kept moving and moving and then the tingling began to lessen. After several minutes, it drained from her body entirely. She no longer felt hot. She sat up.

Lou had placed two things next to her—a glass bottle of Mexican Coke and the same Bluetooth headphones they'd used on Hearing day.

Cara reached for the Coke but the bottle had no surface feeling—the usual strong resistance of touching glass was gone—and no temperature.

What's this? Hearing said. What's this now?

What sensations are you feeling? Lou said from somewhere in the room, possibly high up on the third level. Run through them, Lou said. What can you see? What can you hear? What can you touch? What can you taste? What can you smell?

Cara rubbed her fingers together but there was no result—skin didn't contact skin, there was no touchdown, no resistance or friction. She took a swig of the bottle of Coke and there was no flavor, not even the sensation of liquid in her mouth.

Cara put the headphones on and tapped the right earphone with her fingers. Sounds came on, sounds she recognized as the song from high school she'd been wanting to hear, the one by The Killers about taking off her dress now and letting me go. She could predict the pattern of the notes, up or down, faster or slower, but the music did nothing for her, she felt nothing. No memories came, no images. There was no calm darkness, no sweet bitterness, no fear.

Cara sat very still. She took off the headphones and she—what? Listened. Listened to her body, as people were always saying to do.

But there was nothing. The air conditioner in her mind wasn't just turned off; it was unplugged. Not just unplugged but smashed with a baseball bat. Cara had done that once with that same girl from high school. Drunk on Boone's Farm, they'd hauled an old TV into the girl's hatchback, driven it to a clearing in the woods, rolled it out onto a patchy swath of grass, and smashed it again and again with an aluminum bat. There had been that first moment when the bat made contact with the top of the TV, when its shell was first depressed and then ricocheted back, like a brain being scrambled in its skull.

Inside that unplugged, bashed place—if you have ever been there, then you know—is heaven. Contrary to popular opinion, it is not white but very, very black. There is space there, and some wires, a few harmless sparks. The only sound is a loud but friendly sloshing, like in the beginning of "Champagne Supernova" by Oasis.

I can't feel anything, Hearing said quietly. Then, a moment later, with a kind of wonder: I can't feel *anything*.

Lou? Cara said.

Yes? they answered, from their perch on the top level of the sauna.

What happened to Smell? Did you bring her here too?

Yup, Lou said. Beatrice and I worked here, but not the same work you're doing now. She did a facial instead of a steam, since her problem was the future of her face. She went home early because she was ready to confront the past and didn't want to wait.

And Sight? Cara asked.

Oh. Gin and I did some breathing exercises in the heat,

since her issues were in her lungs. They say sex drive starts in the alveoli.

The grapes? Hearing piped up now. I remember from biology, they always drew the alveoli like fat bunches.

Uh-huh, Lou said. Exactly. Gin's were all hardened like a miner with black lung. But the treatment loosened them right up.

Wow, Cara said.

I know, Lou said.

Cara took off her robe now, just to see, and it was good. Without the sense of the weight and gravity of her apron belly flowing over her upper pussy area, the words *apron belly* and *upper pussy* lost all shame. Without the smell of her armpits, she forgot that her underarm hair was long and thus left behind her ambivalent feelings. She climbed up to the top tier of the sauna and was not hot. Neither was she cold. Her knees did not hurt and she had no fear of falling. She hopped quickly down to the middle level and then to the floor, where she crashed into Hearing, who was conducting his own experiments. They both fell to the ground but were not hurt. When she looked down and raised her leg for inspection, Cara saw that her knee had been scraped and was bleeding a little—just a single rivulet down her shin—but this did not matter.

Wow, Hearing said, also lying naked on the ground. This is fucking amazing. My feet don't hurt anymore. I didn't feel sad when I listened to my ex-wife's and my wedding song.

What song is it? Cara asked.

"Can't Help Falling in Love," Hearing said. The Elvis version, obviously.

Obviously, Cara said.

When Elvis goes *Would it be a sin?,* my ex-wife was walking in and she tripped on her high heel so badly she had to grab on to her uncle's arm and then he helped her keep walking. That image has been burned into me all my life since. I'd see it whenever I listened to that song. But not this time.

Cara knew just what he meant. There was a version of that song by a young woman who'd risen to prominence on YouTube to which Cara's sister had just gotten married. When the singer had sung *Would it be a sin?,* June had appeared alone, partially blocked by a maple tree, in a tea-length A-line dress with a scoop neck made of thick white Spanish crepe. June was neither fat nor thin, but some middle path. She had been raised in the same house as Cara and so was not immune to all that had transpired there, but she had absorbed it differently, moving only a few miles away, choosing a clear career as a large-animal veterinarian, and letting their mother's words dance across her skin and fall off. June's skin that day was bronzed but otherwise unadorned, and as Cara had stood at the end of the aisle with her brother-in-law, she felt that June had made it somewhere, not to the destination of marriage, but to, maybe, the destination of being free. To run from something was not the same thing as being free of it, as it turned out.

Cara smacked her face lightly with her hand but felt nothing.

The door opened then and stayed open.

What is going on here? Anne's voice asked in a low volume

but firm tone. Cara could not see her through the steam, then she could. Anne's hand was all the way inside her big pouf of hair, agitating it.

A specialized experiment, Lou said. One I designed myself. For the treatment-resistant.

No body, Hearing said. None.

Well, we have one, Cara said. We just can't communicate with it.

Stop this now, Anne said.

Through the dissipating steam, Cara could see Lou descending the platforms, coming to stand in front of Anne.

Let them finish, Lou said. It's almost over.

Now, Anne said. Any longer and it could become permanent.

It won't, Lou said. I've timed it out.

You don't know for sure, Anne said. You think you do but you don't.

I do, Lou said. I know that it is worth it. It's the only thing that helped me.

Anne walked over to where Hearing lay on the ground, moving his legs in a kind of frog kick.

Michael, Anne said to him. Please grab my hand and we'll lift you to a sitting position.

Happy, Hearing said. So happy.

This isn't natural, Michael, Anne said. You need to listen to me.

No, Hearing said.

Cara sat up to watch. She saw the arc of his curved belly

and the pinkness of his legs and the floppy strangeness of his penis.

Again Anne said his name.

No! Hearing shouted. I don't want to.

Anne crouched down next to him.

I want you to be well, Anne said. I do. But this is not the way.

More body, Hearing said. More problems.

What about your daughter? Anne said.

She'll understand, Hearing said. And she'll be better off. I think things about her, about her body, that I never say out loud. Terrible things. Things that would harm and scar her. I have worked so hard not to say them. I have never said them. But still, I think them.

Anne turned to Lou.

See what you have done?

It's his choice, Lou said.

Anne moved from Lou to Cara. Again she crouched down, and now they saw eye to eye. She put her hand on Cara's forehead, which Cara could not feel. But it was what her mother used to do.

Cara, Anne said. Are you happy here?

If she was happy, happy was lightness, breath that came in and out. Pressing on a piece of wood and having nothing press back.

I think so, yes, Cara said.

Do you want to stay like this or go back? Anne asked.

Cara had once been a baby who had been born via biology

and science and then loved and wounded via human beings. The residue from the human beings had stuck around, stewed with other leavening juices, and then risen, expanding until it became too large and popped the container of her mind. Then it took over her body, stuffing itself into every nook and cranny, so that it seemed to have originated there. But it was a trick. Cara had been tricked; they all had.

Choose quickly, Cara, Anne said.

Give her a minute, Lou was saying. Let her breathe.

Breathing was a thing that included Cara. Cara was included. Her body had reacted to Lou's sauna just as Hearing's had. It was made of the same stuff. Deep down inside that stuff there was a buzzing now, a pulsing, a little electric spark. The spark caught and revealed a quarry from which everything that was *Cara* was harvested and everything that was *Cara* was grown. It was sweet in there and it was wet and full of sorrow. Cara could touch it the same way she could touch anything. She licked her lips. It was so real, so solid and obvious, this *somethingness* inside her. How could she ever not have known about it?

I'd like to go back, Cara said.

Anne sighed a big sigh and wiped away water from her eyes.

Good girl, Anne said.

Fuck yeah, Lou said, pumping their fist. Did I tell you or did I tell you?

One for two, Anne said. Not so great.

But there's something I need to not forget, Cara said.

What is it? Lou asked.

I can't tell you, Cara said. I can't put it into words.

I think I know what you mean, Anne said.

You do?

I think so. But staying in this room won't help you to not forget it. You'll forget it either way. You'll remember and then you'll forget and then something will happen and you'll remember it again and then you'll forget again.

Cara stood up. She was still naked and she saw Lou and Anne looking but trying not to look at her body.

Then what? Cara asked. Then it just goes on like that forever? How do I remember it if things get bad? If I really need it?

Anne thought. She looked at Lou, then back to Cara. Then Anne spoke: Try.

You need arms and hands to write a story. You could dictate, but that would still require speech, a mouth with its moisture, the tongue and the vocal cords and the breath required to form language. You could blink your eyes in a predetermined system, one blink for *A*, three for *C*, and so on, but you would still need eyes and their lids. There is that French man with locked-in syndrome who wrote a whole book that became a movie this way, blinking more than two hundred thousand times.

From the start of writing this story to the moment of this writing, the body in question aged 2,749 days. It grew larger and then smaller and then larger again. It cried, it is such a crier, with the tears cried during the writing of this story totaling around 480 gallons—enough to fill a fifteen-foot round inflatable pool. Thoughts that went into this story were had: in therapy, a rented space in an office building where the body in question's therapist propped her feet up on a small wooden stool in the shape of an elephant; while walking to and from the corner store to get Diet Coke; while sitting in a hard stadium seat at Citizens Bank Park, home of the Philadelphia Phillies, on buy-one-get-one-free hotdog night; and while in the car commuting to jobs whose performance paid for all these other activities, including the writing of this story.

The body in question got turned on writing the sex scene between Cara and Sight and had to stop several times to masturbate. During the seven and a half years it took to write this story, it had 392 orgasms, became sick with COVID, RSV, regular flu, food poisoning, seasonal allergies, and developed a strange rash between its ring and middle fingers. It ate Pringles and raspberries and roast chicken from the grocery store and Red Baron frozen pizza and fancy restaurant pizza and round yellow tortilla chips straight from the bag. It pushed cats off keyboards and squished the very end of cats' tails down with its thumb to feel that most supple of bones. It became cold and sought comfort under a comforter. Too many times to count did it become gripped with the sudden need to shit—the body in question has IBS—and then shat, thinking about this story while shitting. It went off Celexa and on Trintellix and then off Trintellix and on Zoloft, on Metformin, on Ozempic to decrease its A1C and then off Ozempic because the drug made them sick, on various creams for the finger rash. It took Propranolol to slow its heart rate and Advil for pain and Advil PM and Tylenol PM and Gabapentin for sleep and weed gummies in the flavors Piña Colada, Wild Berry, and Limoncello.

Toward the end of writing this story, the body in question's back seized up so badly that it required five sessions of physical therapy as well as several ninety-minute massages with scented oil in a small, dusty room from two different people, people who in the process of touching the body in question also became bodies in question.

Behind the monitor of the computer used to write this story, one dirty window looked out over a back alley and the backyards of several rowhouses. A small spider crawled across that window; a large water bug, too. Water came in, a nearby electrical wire was severed, and one of the visible backyards was filled with trash, and then emptied. That house was sold and people moved in and put a trash can out there and then filled only the trash can with trash and then emptied it.

And in all that time, the body in question changed. If, at the start, it did not believe that its involvement was necessary for the writing of this story, it is now, here, nearly at the end, able to believe in itself at least enough to ask the question: Without me, where would you be?

ACKNOWLEDGMENTS

Some of these stories were edited and published in earlier forms, and for that labor and care I want to thank Allison Wright and Paul Reyes at *Virginia Quarterly Review,* Halimah Marcus at *Electric Literature,* Adeena Reitberger at *American Short Fiction,* Medaya Ocher at the *Los Angeles Review of Books Quarterly,* Oscar Villalon at *ZYZZYVA,* and Patrick Cottrell and Claire Boyle at *McSweeney's.* Versions of these stories were also workshopped and greatly improved by feedback from Justin Torres and crew at the Lambda Literary Writers Retreat for Emerging LBGTQ+ Voices, and Kelly Link and crew at the Tin House Summer Workshop. These editors and teachers, as well as the independent booksellers who support our work and the people talking about literary fiction on all the websites and all the apps, are the ones ensuring that literature can have a fighting chance of coming with us into the future. Thank you.

Thank you, Helen Thomaides at Hogarth, for your vision and your careful edits, which made this book what it is, and to Parisa Ebrahimi, Maddie Woda, and David Ebershoff, who set us up to play. Enormous thanks to my agent, Jin Auh, who, since the year 2013, never gave up the faith that this book would one day be born, and also to Abram Scharf at Wylie. Thank you to the team at Random House: Peter Dyer, the world's best publicist, who made this book's life better in every way; production editor extraordinaire and gelati lover Cara DuBois; and marketing king and prince Jaylen Lopez and Will Lyman.

Gratitude to Yaddo, Monson Arts, Lighthouse Works, Millay Arts, and the Turkey Land Cove Foundation for the beds, desks, bathtubs, dinners, oceans, forests, fellowship, and time. Thank you to Creative Philadelphia and the U.S. government's Paycheck Protection Program. Thank you, Wesleyan University; the public library of Middletown, Connecticut; and the Free Library of Philadelphia.

Thank you to the real Ray's Happy Birthday Bar, where you really can get a free shot on your birthday. The video art of @wildflower.jasmine enriched the story "Beauty."

Thank you, Hilary Leichter, for your feedback on "Camp Sensation" and on my life, and Denne Michele Norris, for pushing me to always protect my peace. Thank you to my Philly team, the Claw, for whom I will always ride at dawn. Thank you, Alison Fairbrother and Dana Murphy, for secret reasons. Thank you, Mollie Eisenberg, for bringing me into the world of fat liberation; Claire Copley, for teaching me how to see; and Alan Eisenberg, who first gave me short stories. Thank you to my genius therapist, Aleisa Myles. Thank you to my partner, Art Phung, for everything.

If you're a reader who's been burned by depictions of your body in other books, thanks for giving me a chance. I did my best. This book publishes into a lineage of art about bodily experiences that have been seen as disgusting and subhuman; I'm so grateful for that, and may that lineage keep growing ever longer, exploding in volume. It's already happening. It's our world now.

ABOUT THE AUTHOR

EMMA COPLEY EISENBERG is the bestselling author of the novel *Housemates,* nominated for a Lambda Literary Award and the VCU Cabell First Novelist Award, as well as the nonfiction book *The Third Rainbow Girl,* a *New York Times* Notable Book and Editors' Choice and a finalist for an Edgar Award and an Anthony Award. Her fiction, essays, and criticism have appeared in such publications as *Granta, Esquire, Virginia Quarterly Review, The New Republic,* and *The Cut,* and she writes the Substack Frump Feelings. She lives in Philadelphia, where she cofounded Blue Stoop, a community hub for the literary arts.

emmacopleyeisenberg.com
Instagram: @frumpenberg

ABOUT THE TYPE

This book was set in Mercury Text, a family of typefaces designed by Hoefler & Co. The font is available in a series of grades that have different degrees of darkness but share the same character widths.